Grendel

AND OTHER TALL TALES

Grendel

AND OTHER TALL TALES

DUANE HEWITT

PRESSED-TO-TELL PUBLICATIONS • TORONTO

Grendel and Other Tall Tales

This book is a work of fiction. Names, characters, places, and incidents are either products of the author's imagination or are used fictitiously. Any resemblance to actual events, locales or persons, living or dead, is entirely coincidental.

Canadian Cataloguing in Publication Data

Hewitt, Duane, 1958-
Grendel: and other tall tales

ISBN 0-9682200-0-2

I. Title.

PS8565.E899G74 1997 C813'.54 C97-900564-7
PR9199.3.H463G74 1997

Pressed-To-Tell Publications
P.O. Box 455
31 Adelaide Street East
Toronto, Ontario
M5C 2J5

Toll free: 1-888-272-2152

Special thanks to Patrick O'Malley for jacket and book design
Jacket photo: Ken Mulveney, Toronto
Printed and bound in Canada

To the Dreamers...

Grendel and Other Tall Tales

CONTENTS

In dream, delusion, and fantasy, exist man's
next best reality: that place where he is the creator of his
own worlds; where he builds, learns, discovers and entertains;
is master of all outcomes, his own god of destiny,
and thus the student of his own evolving and
ever uncertain truth.

- d.h.

GRENDEL

I will never forget the sound of their screams. Nor will I be free of those horrific and demonic visions: the carnage, the mayhem, broken limbs, shattered bone, the torn and ripped skin. Aye, and that was not the worst of it! There were the sounds; the sounds of men dying; of tearing flesh, of skin ripped away in large ragged swatches, of limbs bent and torn in methods the Lord had not intended. And the screams! The screams! For if it were not enough that man might be subjected to this ungodly cruelty, if it were not already sufficient that men might meet their ends in this most barbaric manner, there was something still far worse. It was the knowing, the dreadful knowing that this horrific demise was, for each man, inescapable.

Oh, that we would have given our very souls to escape the terror! Oh, that there might have been some way to escape the circumstances that led us to the beast; to return, to regress, like frightened little children to a mother who might protect and cajole us. But this was not to be. Forces of dark and despair had other plans for us; plans and visions of a macabre, unworldly intent. For we were led, destined, and manoeuvered into the playground of the beast — the beast Grendel.

And I alone survived.

This is my story...

1848 - East Africa

It had been many weeks that we ventured forth

through this strange and oddly beguiling land — these plains and rainforests of East Africa. Nowhere had I ever before known such a dark and mysterious place. It was a mystical, enchanting land: Ferns of such height that they might reach the highest yardarm, single leaves that could easily engulf a man, crawling bugs and flying insects larger than my hand and of deadlier sorts than the barrel of any musket. This was a place true only to itself, a reality of its own separated by eons of a distinct and singular past, a place where few men had ever dared venture. This was a land that cared for and catered to no one and nothing other than its strange, malevolent self. This, clearly, was not our world.

For many weeks did we toil through the heavy bush, hacking and cutting our trek with the large machetes we had the good foresight to bring. Yet progress was slow. So unforgiving was this jungle, so unsympathetic, it simply did not yield to our presence. Still, we toiled and pushed onward, motivated by our curiosity, our sense of adventure, and by the lust of our greed.

Weeks earlier, our good mother — HMS Lockhart — had set anchor off the eastern coast. So with plans well laid and the assistance of a little luck, seven of us were able to skip ship. Aye, we were ship deserters. And we knew too that the Lockhart's officers would make some attempt to seek us out and bring us to ship's justice. But it was not to be. For our departure — our escape! — was well thought out and executed.

Even though seven men would not be there to ship out again, she could still sail without us, and the remaining men and officers of His Majesty's vessel Lockhart would likely spend little more than five days to a week pursuing us, especially in jungle such as this. After all, this land was much unknown and I knew full well that the officers and crew could not afford the time to seek us out. (God, now that I look back, how I wish we had been caught, no matter the punishment we might have faced.) But we were free, and we made godspeed to our unholy destination.

Forth we went, with the aid of a shoddy map and some faintly remembered directions told me two years earlier. Ah, had it been that long? Two years — and so many worlds ago — that I sat in the seedy underbelly of a tavern halfway across the world, an old ship's captain gone awry, a long night of overimbibing in ale and whisky, and three months' newly earned pay for the information that would lead me here, here on my quest with my shipmates, a quest that would make us rich men — a quest for diamonds!

Yes, diamonds! So often had I heard of the riches that beckoned men to Africa's harsh interior. And so often before had I heard the tales of hardship that befell those who would attempt to bring the stones forth to the world. But I was young and foolhardy. I had survived much in my years, and to be honest and most bold, I felt the winds of grace upon me.

But the journey, we knew, would not be an easy one. What with the heat and the sudden rains that fiercely pounded Africa's jungles, so dense were the downpours it sometimes became most difficult to breathe. A man could almost drown while standing in the open onslaught of such rain. In one of a few cases, the seven of us were left in a frantic struggle for survival against a flash flood and what must have been tons of mud sent flowing from the steep hill-sides that preceded the mountainous range.

And the jungle had its own life's blood, its own code of death and survival. Other than the deep foliage, the immense heat (of which I have scarcely mentioned) and the most difficult terrain, there were the constant sounds of the jungle: Roars, cries, grunts, all of which may have been miles away, and yet frequently seemed to be very close, indeed. Life teemed within the jungle in its own vast assortment of wonders: hierarchies within the food chain.

Onward we trekked, my companions and I, seven souls with a destination. Of those closest to my heart, four stood out as best mates. Tom Lear, the largest and strongest of us all, typically walked the point. A brash man, Tom truly had the eyes of a hawk and all the reflexes to match. He was a large and powerful man and, of all of us, best suited to lead the entourage. Brad Dickens and Gary Laudens had sailed with me before. It wasn't so much that I felt I could trust either of them as much as they were each daring, spiteful men, and with that spirit there was very little they wouldn't do in risking and facing danger. Their spunk was simply the most trustworthy aspect of their personalities. Finally, John Masters and myself, each of us somewhat introverted, but John possessed the inner strength of a Buddhist monk and the physical endurance of a bull.

With muskets, machetes and as much gear as we could get away with, we marched onward, sleeping at night as best as possible, all the time feeling the presence of life and mystery around us.

On one of the late afternoons before setting camp, we were all startled by a great shrieking and commotion coming through the trees. We headed toward the sounds straightaway. As we entered a less dense area of bush, we realized that the near-human cries came from a great community of chimpanzees. They were so taken up with the focus of their attention that they hadn't noticed our approach. Scattered through the trees, both at the highest points and right down to the ground, were as many as 50 chimps. Only then, after stopping to observe, did we take in the drama at hand. Many of the larger and more agile of the chimpanzees were practically flying through the treetops in pursuit of several other monkeys — monkeys that were not of the chimp family. In less than a moment after our appearance on the scene, several (of what I think were male) chimpanzees had caught the smaller monkeys and immediately began ripping and tearing the monkeys apart, near eating them alive! As this occurred, the remainder of the chimps were quick to gather at the base of the trees where the captures had taken place. Immediately, remains of the dead monkeys were tossed to the ground where they were quickly and eagerly consumed by the group.

We had just witnessed a most gruesome, and yet fantastic, hunt. We silently slipped backward and made haste from the witnessed blood feast and on again toward our destination.

On yet another occasion, we had a near altercation with one of the jungle's big cats. It was Gary who was quickest with his musket: The leopard had not quite begun to leap when it was laid to rest by a single blast of gunpowder and lead.

It was far into the journey, after we had reached the steep hillsides, much deeper within the mountainous rock and caverns, that we were aware a change had occurred. In retrospect, it seemed an almost intangible quality, a subtle difference had overcome us since leaving the jungle. But there was definitely a change, unidentifiable (at first) though it was.

John was first to decipher the strange difference. Although this might seem clear and obvious, I can't quite say why it was so hard for us to determine. For it was silence! And an eerie silence indeed that surrounded us, but moreover it was the absence of life itself. True, true — for as we had first ascended into the rocky hills, there came a point where we realized that the cliffs and rocks — though still on the verge of the jungle — were completely void of the vast assortment of life we had left behind only a short while ago.

And it was the most incredible kind of silence, a nerve-racking quiet of a shattering sort, the type of quiet that might drive a man mad, or stir the most confident and savage of beasts. So very strange it was, as if something deep within and unseen gave the hills and jungle pause, as if in waiting. These periods of quiet were the most frightening, the most eerie, and the hardest to account for.

Nonetheless, we continued; upward and onward, hiking into the mountain range that once arrested our eyes from the horizon. Deeper we went, into the rocky abyss.

And that was when we heard it.

It was on the third night of making camp within the rocks that we were startled awake by that horrendous, inhuman scream: A bloodless, gut-wrenching scream that transformed into a howl of such piercing and high-pitched intensity, it seemed to both emanate from and penetrate the very rock itself. I still remember it all so well. John was first to react.

"Listen mates," John exclaimed. "What in God's name is that?"

"Shut up!" Tom wailed. "Listen!"

"That ain't no cat," Brad said. "Ain't no ape neither."

It continued endlessly. I can only say it was the single most inhuman sound I have ever heard.

Contrary to what one might think would be a natural instinct to this awesome sound, (and although we did at first shrink from it) it is interesting to note that the men were intent on knowing from whence the screams came. I can only compare this curious behavior of ours to the way one both withdraws from, and yet is attracted to, fire.

The hellish screams continued, and as nerve-shattering as they were, we grew more and more intent on discovering the source, for this was not the sound of any large cat we might have known. I wondered if it might have been some sort of ape.

"Hell no," one of the others shouted. "That's nothin' o' the sort."

"Listen," I said. "Does it sound like there's more than one?"

"Nah," Gary said. "There's just one o' whatever is makin' that sound."

Sure enough, it seemed to be a scream emitted by one creature only, and I might add we were driven by our fear and curiosity.

Yet, because it was the middle of the night and we were in treacherous hills and rocks unknown to us, there was no way we could have safely strayed from the camp. And with the dark, what did we really think we might find? Sensibly, we returned to camp shortly after the sounds faded and we made efforts to return to sleep — though, in truth, I think few of us had any real sleep from that point onward into the dawn.

We gathered together in the early part of the morning and again continued our trek, following our map and feeling very much on course. By all estimations, we hoped to arrive within the rocky caverns that housed our riches within the next few days.

As one might guess, all conversation centered on speculation of what had disturbed our sleep that night. The mystery would only deepen.

We hiked onward and upward, and again, the going was slow and difficult. Fortunately, some elements of the deep bush still existed into the rocky hills, so we were able to help ourselves to various berries as well as to the water from numerous streams and springs. It was about five miles along from the point of our night camp that we made a most bizarre discovery, a discovery which only added to our befuddlement of the earlier night's sounds. Every man felt a connection between the haunting screams and our new discovery.

We had stumbled upon several mutilated wildebeest carcasses, in a place where wildebeests should not be. Our elevation was too high, the going too rough for this grazing, African-type buffalo to habitat. And surely, no lion or other predatory cat would be equipped to carry wildebeest carcasses from the killing plains so many miles and days behind us.

But it wasn't just the presence of the mutilated carcasses that puzzled us. No — there was something far stranger, and upon examination, more terrifying.

Embedded in one of the carcasses, impressed within the very meat and bone of this huge buffalo, was the largest animal track — a footprint!

Aye, though not complete was it. For whatever beast had stepped into the wildebeest's carcass, only a good half of the foot made the impression, but it was unmistakable. Much like a human's or perhaps an ape's foot, it had one large toe like a man's, but with only two slightly smaller toes next to it. Farther down and set to the left was yet another large appendage, separate and almost claw-like. To the farthest right of the imprint was another smaller little toe or claw. Overall, the width of the imprint would have been two feet across. The length we couldn't determine, for as I stated, only the first half or third of the foot was imprinted in the wildebeest's body: The surrounding ground was shale rock, so there were no other imprints that we could see.

But the very weight of those carcasses! What creature could have carried them, for each must have weighed well over 1,200 pounds! And carried them we assumed it must, for no wildebeest lived in these parts.

Each man's eyes gazed at the scene, then slowly, each man looked around at one another and finally all eyes settled on me. The tension was thick as a Tyne fog.

"What the bloody 'ell are we gonna do now?" Brad asked.

"Aye to that," Tom said, turning to me. "This ain't somethin' anyone's ever come across before."

"At least not and have come back to talk about," I agreed.

After some pause, we loaded the muskets and voted to move on.

We continued the journey, this time, however, we were

much more intent upon our surroundings, for we were interested in knowing if we might find other footprints.

We found nothing.

Again we continued. Moving at what seemed an increase in elevation, the journey was nothing easier. The air had definitely changed, and as we again approached evening, the temperature was clearly a great deal cooler — a stark difference, by comparison, to the heat during the day. As for the mood of the men and the state of our nerves, what fool would not be apprehensive about what we had seen and heard to this point in our journey? I can only say that, intuitively, I never felt we had left the danger behind us, and what was more frightening, I felt we had an unseen presence accompanying us from a distance — a presence which was most unwanted.

As day came to a close, it was clear that we would again have to establish camp. Through one of our descents down a rather steep hill, we had observed a spot on the other side of a deep gorge where we thought we might find shelter and a place to finally give in to the day's strains.

Approaching the gorge, it became evident that we would have to cross a rather slim ledge, a dangerous precipice that extended a good 50 yards in length over a deep culvert which rose 800 feet above a rocky formation. Although we estimated it might take as long as a half hour to cross the precipice, it did in fact take over an hour, due to the tedious and arduous nature of the crossing.

No mishaps occurred, however, and for that we were all grateful. Having reached the other side, we were able to establish camp under a large rocky overhang. Behind us, the rock tapered downward into a slit where loose shale was sandwiched between two large slabs of rock, no more than 18 to 20 inches wide. Before us was the vast chasm, and a sheer drop downward.

The men finally settled down into the evening. A fire was set to warm ourselves and we sang into the dusk to ease our spirits and our nerves. None of us spoke of our apprehension, but there wasn't a man in the group who did not think it. For although we had walked well for a day, our distance travelled was not all too far, and so it was that we each carried with us the sounds of the night before, and the strange scene of the mutilated carcasses of the wildebeests.

The stars shone beautifully with a near full moon overhead, and we all finally fell into a deep slumber, both from our physical exhaustion as well as from the titillation of our raw, nervous anxieties. The night air cooled considerably, and one would not have thought that the nights anywhere on this vast continent could be so cool, in contrast to the heat of the days. Yet, it was all so beautiful, and so very surreal. We slept as exhausted men sleep, each falling into the sweet caress of his own, personal state of dreams.

Somewhere in the dead of night came that rude awakening.

I think only a few of us awoke at first. For shortly

after we had fallen into a most peaceful sleep, sounds of a great commotion — a struggle! — came from an area near one of the men.

What I saw that night still makes my blood run cold. Outlined in the moonlight was the silhouette of some huge, grotesque, man-like thing. And though it was bent over the bodies of one of the men, I could see that it was indeed enormous, yet not ape-like in appearance nor in the way it moved. As my mind came alert and my eyes focused on the scene, I felt nauseated at what I was witnessing. As the thing crouched over one of the bodies of the men, I could now see that the monstrous wretch was devouring our man like a meal! So intent was it, it had not noticed that we others were awakening. Pulling and tearing at its victim's flesh, it consumed its meat with great concentration.

As the reality became lucid in my mind, I began screaming.

"Hey! Jesus! Tom! TOM, JOHN!"

As the others awoke to the terror of the scene, we all began screaming, waving, and throwing rocks at the thing, hoping to scare it away. The beast, startled from its bliss, reeled back and stood erect. Although in the dim light I could not make it out in detail, the shadow and outline of the monster was clear enough.

The beast was awesome in size, for it must have stood 12 feet high when it stood erect. And much like a man it was, with two legs and two arms, aye, and it was the arms that seemed to create the greatest awe about the creature; they were long, long enough that they might reach the ground though he stood straight up. And muscular! Yet, I say it was not ape-like, this was something unknown. It was a creature of its own kind.

So startled were we that we, in turn, had startled the beast. It was here that it let out that wretched wail we had heard nights before. So piercing. Such a loud shriek and howl. And with this demonic scene to which we awoke, the howl was enough to chill a man's blood. We froze in our tracks from the sound of the thing, and then, before we had a chance to reach for muskets or light a fire, the thing spun and was gone.

How might I describe the feelings of the men? How might I say what the night was like from there on? Of heaven and Earth, what could prepare a man for this thing we had fallen upon? There is no way to describe our true feelings.

We stood staring at the scene where the thing had left. Frozen in our steps with minds racing. Finally, after moments that seemed like hours, we began lighting fires, again checking our muskets and drawing out machetes. Who could know if the beast might return to us. As the minutes passed, the extreme anxiety and fright of the men gave way to a great deal of nervous muttering and speculation.

My heart wrenched when I saw that the poor bastard who had been killed was John: He had been half devoured. Nausea overwhelmed me and I fell to my knees and retched. Much like the wildebeests we saw earlier, he had been torn apart. This was not the way things were supposed to go for us, and I was suddenly struck by the seriousness of our predicament and by the loss of a friend. God willing, I hope he died quickly.

That night I wept, though I kept it to myself. Morning came and I needn't say that none of us slept in waiting for the dawn.

We had to gather ourselves and decide what was best for the group, as well as what each man wanted. Clearly, turning back was an option but not one any of us wanted to consider. We had spent weeks coming as far as we did, and by all accounts we were probably very close to our goal — an area, as marked by the map, which would be deep and cavernous and which would actually lead downward from the elevation we now held.

Despite the tragedy we had experienced, the consensus was that we would continue. In truth, each man knew we had little choice. Dangers were a part of our expedition, that was something we understood from the beginning. And although this demon was something unknown, we all agreed it was still a beast, and must be subject to the laws of life and death in the jungle.

We therefore checked, yet again, all muskets and made sure extra gun powder was at the ready. With machetes in hand, we would continue as before, but would try to double our pace. Furthermore, we stayed tighter as a group and planned not to let any man out of sight of another. Flints were also at hand, which were intended to give us the chance to light a fire or torch. With little else to do, we buried John's remains, covering him with shale, sand and rock. Few of us said anything during the burying that served as a ceremony. We then made our way.

Though we spoke very little, each man must have pondered just what that monster was. One could not help but wonder if we were being watched, like a little flock of sheep due for slaughter.

That must have been the longest day of the entire journey. Yet it was uneventful, for with the exception of sighting and slaughtering a wild boar, we saw little of any creature that day.

We made good time and began our descent into the cavernous rock. With luck, we would find the end of our journey by mid-afternoon of the next day. But for now, we would have to settle into one of the caverns and again establish camp.

It was on each man's mind that we find a cave where we could set up camp, someplace from which we could defend and protect ourselves should the beast return. We passed various small caves and overhangs of rock, but nothing as ideal as we hoped to find.

Finally, toward late afternoon, we discovered a deep cavern which seemed to be the closest ideal. The cavern itself was not too deep within the rock, in fact, we had only to climb down an eight or nine-foot escarpment of shale to reach the inner beginnings of the cave. It occurred to us that such a cave might already be inhabited by other animals, be it cats or wild boars, but as we entered with lit torches it did indeed seem free of any life.

With every man now carrying a fully lit torch, we were able to examine what was to become our stopover. The cave continued deep into the back of the rock, and sloped downward to a point where it contained a small pool of water. The cave itself produced a huge maw once deep within it, with a ceiling that arched a full 20 to 25 feet overhead. The inner width of the cave may have been 50 to 60 feet across, and as I stated, it continued a good 75 to 80 feet back before it reached the pond. The pond itself was the full width of the cave at that rear portion, and continued for an additional 30 feet before meeting the cave wall. Having smelled and tasted the water, I can say that it was not stagnant, even though it had a very hard taste — doubtless from the rock and mineral influence. But for its degree of freshness, it had to have been spring-fed.

In some portions of this new dwelling, the cave walls were like hard granite, yet other walls were again shale. Some areas provided inner little overhangs and small cavities where a man, or an animal, might crawl for added shelter. We checked every crevice and cavity and found no reason not to stay. Although there was no other way out other than the main entry, it did seem defendable, should it come to that, and we certainly had room to move and stretch out in our new night-time habitat.

We gathered dry firewood and kindling to keep us

warm and our premises well lit. Dark clouds had been gathering during the last bit of light that day and we expected a downpour. As evening set in, huge thunderclaps shook the rock, which seemed most ominous, but the rains never came.

We ate well that night, having roasted the wild pig we were able to kill earlier. Then came the time for us to make plans for our night. It would not do to have all the men sleeping should that beast, or the likes of it, discover our whereabouts.

A group decision was made that two men would keep watch at the mouth of the cave at all times during the night. Both would keep watch for a two-and-a-half-hour period, then they would wake two others, who in turn would take over the watch. In this manner, all six men would have both slept and contributed to the watch. We would each have received a somewhat disturbed five hours of rest over a seven-and-a-half-hour period. It was also wise to have two men up together at each time to prevent the other from falling into slumber.

The two youngest lads volunteered to begin the shift, and the remaining four of us withdrew to the back of the cave and quickly found sleep.

We must have slept for close to two hours, but we were startled awake by the fiercest of screams and a great commotion.

The damnable beast was back.

The four of us awoke to the scene of a living hell. This was a nightmare I would always remember. The two men, youths they were really, were being preyed upon by the monster. And they died in agonies I can even now scarce believe. As the creature held one at bay by pinning him down with its great leg, it held, at arms length, the other and glared into the man's eyes. Then, with a ferociousness unaccountable to God, it ripped the man's right arm right out of its socket and drank the blood from the limb! Both men were hysterical, one from the pain and knowledge of the onset of death, the other from the sheer terror of the scene. The beast threw the remains of the arm far to the side, then bent inwards with its great jaw, and tore out the throat of the already semiconscious man.

Then, with a great coldness, we could see in the starlight how it let the twitching corpse fall to the rock, and beheld once again with cold, dark eyes its second victim. With a great scream and cruel, massive strength, it systematically and sadistically tore each limb from the hellishly screaming man. As if this were not enough, it then ripped the remainder of the torso in half, and literally licked the blood from its hands.

For much of the scene, the remainder of us stood, unbelieving, with eyes affixed on the nightmare before us. This was a thing that to face would take a courage much beyond any of us. Gary and Brad ran to the back of the cave seeking refuge — themselves on the verge of hysterics. Tom, God bless him, with ice in his veins, grabbed a musket and let fire a blast directly at the beast. Meanwhile, I was quick to light a torch, lest we all be fumbling in the dark.

Whether Tom missed or the musket was simply not felt by the monster I cannot say, but it had no effect, other than driving the thing into a greater rage. It bent low and peered in at us through the cave's opening, and let out a series of wild, fierce screams. It was that dreadful sound we had all heard before, and with what we had just witnessed, it paralyzed us.

I, too, reached for a musket and fired but my aim was off, for I was shaking and not in full charge of my senses. I screamed for Gary and Brad to return and help us battle the thing, but I could not blame them for their reactions. Their fear had taken over where intelligence might govern.

Tom and I were both frantically reaching for the two other loaded muskets to fire at it again, but the thing had gone. Once again, in our heightened sense of anxiety, the whole incident seemed to be over as quickly as it had begun. Suddenly, all was very quiet — but the screams of the beast and the dying men seemed to reverberate in my mind. Neither Tom nor I had the courage to approach the opening of our cave, lest the thing be nearby.

And no sooner had we been engulfed in this momentary silence than we heard a great thud near the mouth of our cave. The beast was still with us! And it was dropping a huge boulder at the foot of our one exit out of the cave!

"It's trying to seal us in!" Tom screamed. "Grab the muskets, start firing. Hurry!"

We quickly began shouting and firing our muskets,

but it was no use. The beast rolled the great boulder against the opening of our cave, locking us in as its prey! I will never forget the moment before the great rock sealed us in, for the beast stuck its hideous head within and gazed at us with cold, black eyes, and then screamed, as if from its bowels. We covered our ears, for its howl was both deafening and numbing. It then proceeded with its task, sealing us in, and we could hear it throwing rock and sand against the giant boulder and forever sealing us in our tomb!

Then, there was silence, total and deafening as only a pure, cold silence can be. It was the darkest part of the night, and as shattered as our nerves were, we had to collect ourselves and prepare for the inevitable, the monster's return.

"Brad, Gary," I screamed. "Get back here, we need you here now!"

We needed the strengths of one another, and it was important that we keep our wits about us. Tom was a lot less understanding about the reaction of the other two men. Hollering remarks of cowardice at them, he vowed he'd drag them both out and sacrifice them to the creature if they did not come join us.

Their hysteria subsided and they returned. Brad was the first to exclaim when he saw the closed entry:

"Wha'? — we're trapped! That thing's trapped us in here!" he wailed.

"That's the damn truth," Tom said bluntly.

"Well, what for?" Brad persisted. "What's it wanna trap us in here for?"

"What the bloody 'ell do you think?" Tom fired off. "We're fodder for that bloody thing! We're dinner!"

"Like fish in a barrel," Gary offered.

"Fish in a barrel," Tom agreed.

We lit yet another torch, rebuilt our camp's fire to a small blaze, and loaded each of the muskets. No one would sleep any more this night. But in reality, what were we to do? Although there were four of us, we were like fleas to the strength and ferocity of the beast. Clearly, we had to think of a way to escape, for none of us had the will nor desire to confront it.

Yet, in each of our hearts, we knew that a confrontation was likely unavoidable, for we were now its captives. We also knew from the time we first surveyed our cave that there was only the one entry. With the heavy rock now blocking our only way out, we had to assume that the beast was outside the cave. Nonetheless, we began searching the back of the cave, looking for any crevice or passageway out of our tomb.

But we found nothing.

We examined all available alternatives. Since there was no other way out, we were left with one exit. Could we move the boulder from the mouth of the cave? Clearly, we would have to try. And the beast? It became apparent that we would find ourselves in a position of direct contact with the demon. But we did not have sufficient weapons to deal with a monster of such size and strength. We would have to do the best we could, and hope to get away. Everything would come down to pure speed and aggression on our part. In truth though, it would be everyone for himself.

Each man loaded and prepared his musket. As well, each prepared sacks with water and small amounts of food that we had with us. Whatever was going to happen, we had to be ready to make a break for it. And whether we were able to move the boulder, or the beast returned and did it for us, we would likely splinter as a group and do our best to escape.

Tom and I both had our eyes on Brad and Gary. At this point, both seemed somewhat subdued but in control. Still, Tom and I exchanged looks, and I think we both knew that neither of the two men would be their own best bet for survival. And yet, I always thought them to be fearless men.

After several hours and having not heard any sounds of the beast, we steadied ourselves and approached the rock. Whether the thing waited outside or not, we had to take the chance and risk leaving the cave, provided we could move the boulder.

The four of us approached the boulder and began applying our strength to move it.

And that was as far as we got.

The fact that we could barely budge the rock didn't matter. The beast was directly outside, and was now alerted to our movements and our attempts to break free. It obliged us and moved the boulder for us.

With one wild scream, the boulder was cast aside by a mere couple of feet by the monster. Immediately, a huge savage arm reached in and grabbed Brad, who began shrieking in panic. The three of us eased around the rock just in time to see Brad die. In the twilight, we could see the thing grasp a massive claw-hand around Brad's head and rip it clean away from his body. The monster then upended the headless body and drank down the blood.

The three of us opened fire immediately. At least two of our shots hit the thing square in the chest. But that hardly seemed to daunt it. Screaming wildly, it threw Brad's body to the side and made a swipe at us. It missed each of us. With another swipe it near caught Tom. Yet, with a great stride, it stepped over and pinned Gary. With sadistic glee, it began twisting and breaking every limb of the screaming, hysterical man! Tom and I were quick to reload our muskets. But before we could complete the load and fire, it glared at us with cold, challenging eyes, and then bent over and plunged a great fist into Gary's body, eviscerating the man right before our eyes.

With muskets now loaded, we levelled our weapons and fired. My blast caught the beast directly in its right shoulder, to which it let out a hellish screech. But Tom's weapon misfired, and that was his undoing. For as the thing realized that Tom was briefly undefended, it strode directly in front of Tom and stood before him. Tom, fearless as he was, swung the musket and caught the beast in the jaw. As the thing reached in and hoisted Tom up to its eye level, it peered intensely at its prey.

There was little I could do. There was never time to reload the musket, so I took my machete and ran forward, hacking at the beast's legs. Tom had made an effort to reach his machete, but the beast had pinned Tom's arms to his side as he was hoisted six feet off the ground.

How can I describe this scene? Everything seemed to speed by so fast, and yet for some moments, time was still.

I saw Tom, held at eye level to the great beast who was clearly gloating before the kill. I saw Tom's face, in a cold sweat, his eyes fearful and knowing he was about to die.

"Tom!" I screamed, not knowing what to do, "I..."

"Run!" Tom screamed. "RUN!"

And that was the last thing I heard Tom scream before he was torn, limb from limb.

And God forgive me, I did run. While Tom was dying his horrendous death, and knowing I could not fight the beast alone, I used that moment to make good my escape. So I ran, and I ran, and I ran. To the echoing screams of Tom's lingering death, I ran!

Up through the rocky escarpment, and along the trails that we had come just a day earlier, I ran in terror like a child runs in a nightmare. Was the thing behind me? I didn't know. The more I ran the more the terror struck me. But I thanked God for the moonlight that now shone and the stars that let me find my way. Though I stumbled often, I was powered by the adrenaline of my fears.

After several hours, dawn began to break.

I continued, stopping only once to rest and consume what food I had with me. Who could know when I would have a chance to eat again? I no longer ran, but I paused from time to time to listen for signs of the creature, but I heard and saw nothing.

By retracing our original path, I was able to make very good time. And I was still very much fuelled by nervous energy. Before the sun was directly overhead, I was approaching our previous camp, facing the gorge, where John had died.

Knowing I could not continue much further without additional rest and nourishment, I made the decision to stop. I also realized that I had the precipice before me, and I knew I couldn't make it across without gathering some energy.

As I came around the bend and approached the rocky overhang, I was struck with that feeling of merciless defeat and nausea that only a dying man can feel.

The beast, panting and bleeding, lay waiting at the junction of the rocky base where the path over the gorge met the rock. I had nowhere to run.

I had to think. I couldn't turn back, for I would lack for food and surely die of hunger and exposure. Plus, if it had been tracking me or knew that I would return to this spot, then it likely could close in on me if I did backtrack. I had nowhere else to go, and for me to leave this rock, I had to return over the precipice. The beast was injured, however, and I didn't know how seriously. It may have been crippled and slowed by its wounds, but as with many wounded animals, it likely had its own will and strength for survival and retribution.

I had no option. I would have to risk walking directly by the thing and crossing to the other side of the gorge.

I proceeded slowly. It was almost funny in a strange way; like a small child trying to sneak past the sleeping parent or the family dog. The reality, of course, was far more serious, the consequences for failure — lethal.

My breath pounded in my head. I felt I could not quiet or sustain a relaxed demeanour, and my heart felt like it was ready to burst from my chest. So loud did my heartbeat seem, so cold was the sweat that covered me, but bit by bit I inched forward until I was directly before the thing. Its breathing was very deep and consistent as it slept, and I was so close now I could smell the creature's vile odour. But I kept moving.

Then, quite suddenly and without warning, the thing began to stir. I froze in my tracks, holding out for the chance that it would not awaken.

With a guttural sigh, it awoke and sat up erect, staring directly at me as if slow to realize the fact of my presence before it. With eyes affixed on mine, it slowly rose to its feet, half bent over and with its massive arms extended, as if to catch a mouse that was ready to scurry away.

Yet, I had wasted no time. For while the thing was coming to, I had readied and aimed my musket at the thing's chest, and fired!

It wailed and actually fell back! And I knew that from the previous night it must have been weakened. I had to act quickly. Do I make a go for it across the rocky overpass above the gorge? Or do I back track to the overhang where we had established camp just two nights ago? The creature was still able to move, if I chose to retreat to the previous camp site where I might hide under the slates of great rock I had seen there before, the thing might never give up on me. And if it couldn't get at me there, it would only have to wait as I slowly died for lack of food and water. Yet on the precipice over the gorge before me, it would still take me a half hour to cross, and as big as the creature was, I never doubted that it could follow me, even with its wounds.

I went for the gorge!

It was the only option I had. In the few seconds I had before the beast could rally itself, I was on the steep cliff making my escape. Again, I was fuelled by my fear. But, by God, I had a chance. Having crossed the precipice once before with my companions, I knew I could do it, must do it, in quicker time. Throwing caution to the wind, I made my best speed. And I knew, too, if death were to be my only escape from this nightmare, then I would rather die in the fall than at the hands of that hideous beast.

Foot by desperate foot, I made my way; chest

pressed close to the rock and musket and gear slung over my shoulder. I was less than 15 feet over the edge when the thing began threatening me with its unearthly scream, trying to grab at me with its far-reaching arms. Despite its wounds, it still had plenty of life and fight in it. The howls and shrieks continued, with a numbing and sickening effect that could only be a prelude to death. Then, with a surprising display of ingenuity, the beast had found a long, dried tree branch and was trying to knock me from the face of the cliff!

But I continued. I was now 25 to 30 feet from the start of the cliff, and the thing abandoned the branch and began throwing rocks at me. It would not give up! By pure chance, none of the small boulders hit me, which may have been more due to the beast's injured state than anything else. I was now a good 50 feet from the edge and the angry creature.

I knew I had a chance of making it!

Then came the one thing I wouldn't have expected, the last thing I could have wanted, it stepped onto the ledge to pursue me. Lord God, if I ever needed you, now was the time. I had 30 yards to go, and with that thing's great stride, despite its massive size on the small ledge, it would doubtless reach me before I made it to the other side.

I had to keep going. There was nothing else I could do. I had no room to try to reload the musket, and I would certainly not have the time with that thing so close behind me. Step by step I made my way. I could swear I heard it breathing, as it too, pressed close against the rock. My mind began to race. Was there anything else I could do? I considered trying to knock away a portion of the ledge where I had just crossed, but there just wasn't enough time.

I now had less than 20 yards to go, and the creature was gaining on me. Even if I did reach the other side, I would have to run and try to find time to reload my musket. Would I even have time to run? Would there be time to reload? I decided I would deal with one moment at a time.

As I came closer to the final 10 yards, the thing began its horrible scream. The beast was now less than five yards away from me and I began to feel that I just wasn't going to make it. It was closing quickly and I would soon be within its grasp. I decided that when I thought the moment was upon me, I would jump for the final end of the precipice and risk the fall to death should I not make it.

As my pulse raced and both the end and the creature seemed to be each within contact, I resigned myself for the worst. I felt a well of anger rise up within me as I realized just how close I really came. But I was still too far from the end to risk the jump, and the creature was a moment away from reaching me. How cruel life can be, I thought, as a thousand different visions and regrets raced through my mind about the life I'd lived and how I came to face my own death in this nightmarish situation.

I was still young and I didn't want to die.

Something within me screamed out to survive! But fate had other plans for me. I would die like my companions, either at the hands of this monster or by the fall, and just when I was so close to the possibility of sanctuary.

I could now smell the stench of the wretched thing closing in on me, and I knew it would soon reach out for me at any moment. With just five yards to go and still many feet over the gorge, I now had no choice — I would have to jump for it.

I said my prayers and held true contempt for the greed in my soul that led me to this land.

Then, as I briefly closed my eyes and readied myself for the leap that I could not possibly make, I heard that unmistakable sound — flintlock!...

And, the immediate sound of rifle fire! Rifles! I spun my head to see that unmistakable and now most welcome scene. One of the Lockhart's officers and two of her crew were firing rifles at the beast! — at the beast!

The Lockhart had sent a small party in pursuit of us after all. And now, they were here, with rifles! — more sure and more deadly than the muskets we had made off with. Shot after shot rang out as I pressed against the rock. Shot after shot hit the damnable thing.

And then, with one final great scream; a howl of torment and pain, it fell from the cliff to the bottom of the gorge far below — dead.

And I was saved.

Sussex, England - 1860

It has now been 12 years since my rescue from that encounter in Africa.

I was brought to justice and punished severely, as all deserters are, upon my return to the Lockhart. Yet, I sailed with His Majesty's Navy for several more years before finally giving it up and leaving.

I now work and live job to job, day to day, grateful for every blessed moment.

"The Land of Heorot," my mother told me once as a young child, was where the great Beowulf defeated the most savage of all beasts — Grendel.

Well, one thing I know: No Beowulf am I, but then again, I have lived to tell of a thing far more real and far more terrifying than that of any fable.

And life has never tasted so sweet.

THE MAN WHO FELL FOREVER

This is a tale which may lead you to think me mad. But as God is my judge, I swear it is true. And if madness were a haven from anguish, a retreat for solace, it is to such a place I would go, wishing myself godspeed, rather than face that which is as true as I know myself to be sane.

I had spent my last two seasons of skydiving at Slipstream Adventures, or, as is known in more affectionate terms, The EZ-DZ. I still qualified as something of a beginner in the activity of sport parachuting, which I began only five years, and nearly 300 jumps, ago. The school is one of several in the world that specializes in AFF training. AFF is short for Accelerated Free Fall, a course which refers to the advancement of the student from the time they make their first jump to the point at which they may skydive unsupervised. AFF is a method of training, not the rate of speed at which you fall.

Slipstream is also the kind of place where a great camaraderie can be found among the jumpers. Unlike so many sports where you are little more that just a number, out here you are one of the gang. For this reason, many jumpers of varying degrees of experience come to enjoy and improve upon their sport, and in many cases engage in what is known as "relative work."

Relative work is the term used when a number of skydivers participate in free-fall manoeuvres together. Much like water ballet, a group of typically four or more jumpers will leave the aircraft at a considerable height, (usually about 10,000 feet or so, depending on the aircraft being used and the existing weather conditions), and will then perform synchronized movements before arriving at the altitude where each will release his pilot chute and therefore the main canopy, in preparation for a safe landing.

Well, it was on such a jump that this bizarre tale begins. I had been skydiving for much of the summer, and was involved in a number of jumps, typically with five others, all the time performing relative work exercises. In my case, I am the least experienced of the others with whom I was making the dives. I am only now approaching my 300th jump, whereas all of the others have 2,000, and in some cases even 3,000, jumps to their credit.

All, that is, except Jason. Jason is also experienced, and more so than me, but in his case he still hasn't quite made it to that milestone 1,000th jump. For on this one day in early September, he was making his 800th jump and was celebrating doing so with the five of us in our free-fall formation.

There is actually very little to say about that particular day or the events that led up to the dive. It was the long weekend in September and quite a beautiful sunny Saturday. Bob was the most senior and experienced skydiver among us, and therefore the team jump master. We began our routine by doing some "dirt diving," which is really just a form of rehearsing the exit and the free-fall manoeuvres on the ground.

We went through the rehearsal a number of times to make sure each man knew the drill. It wouldn't do to have any confusion once you were hurtling toward the Earth at 120 mph. You had to know exactly where you were supposed to be and when, and you had to know the sequence of movements.

Once we all agreed we had it down, and with Bob's okay, the pilot was notified to start the engines and prepare for take-off. We were fortunate that particular weekend, for we had the use of a Cessna Caravan, a double-prop aircraft with a side exit which can hold up to 14 jumpers. It also has the advantage of being big enough to gain just a bit more altitude than a smaller plane. With this aircraft, we could make jumps from 12,000 and 12,500 feet. With the six of us aboard, we would exit the aircraft at the altitude of 12,500, and have a full 50 seconds of free-fall before we ceased manoeuvres at 4,000 feet, and broke off to open our chutes above 2,400 feet.

Everything went by the book. At approximately 12:30 p.m., we took off in ideal weather. After just over 20 minutes, we had arrived at our altitude of 12,500 feet. As team jump master, Bob did the spotting to direct the pilot over the drop zone and then notified the pilot to stall the engines, which would slow the plane's speed enough for our safe exit. Bob asked if we were ready to jump, to which he received an enthusiastic assortment of affirmations. We collectively took our positions in the exit, and out we fell. Within six seconds we were each stable, falling at terminal speed of 120 mph in our respective positions, and so our relative exercises now began.

Again collectively, we all went through the movements without a hitch, and it was clear from the smiles and grins on each man's face, especially Bob's, that by this point we were all quite happy with the drop. And so it was that we completed manoeuvres by 4,000 feet and each fell away on our own in order to deploy our canopies above the required 2,400 feet.

As we approached 2,600 feet, you could see, one by one, canopies being deployed and each man being rapidly slowed in his rate of descent as main chutes opened. I held out for just a second or two more and opened right at 2,400 feet. It was here that I noticed, just before deploying my chute, that Jason went speeding by me, grinning and waving away. I thought nothing of it, thinking he would likely deploy somewhere under 2,400 feet. As my canopy developed and flapped overhead, I enjoyed the view around me and casually coasted downward in a gentle spiral, all the time conscious of keeping a safe distance from my peers, who were also in slow descent.

I landed among the others, having shouted the standard "clear" before touching down. There was some degree of laughter and chatter as we each gathered our chutes and began walking back to the trailer area of parked cars just 20 yards from where we had touched down.

Then, as if the realization occurred to each of us at the same moment, we all noticed that there were five men who had landed, not six.

"Where's Jason?" someone called out. Sure enough, the five of us spun around looking across the 30-acre field encircling us, trying to see where Jason might have come down.

"He whizzed right by me at 2,400," I volunteered. "But he was smiling and waving all the time."

"Did you see him deploy?" Bob asked.

"No," I responded. "But there was definitely no indication of trouble, he seemed fine."

We approached some of the spectators, girlfriends mostly, who were situated by the cars and picnic benches in the area fenced off from the actual drop zone. We asked if anyone had seen where the sixth jumper, Jason, had come down. No one had seen anything.

At the altitude where he would have had to "pull," it was agreed that he couldn't be too far away. It was possible that he may have coasted into the tree line around the field. We gave it five minutes, just in case he was already walking back, but still, no Jason.

We agreed to undertake a search to locate him. It was, after all, possible that he might have been hurt in the landing, and if he were hurt or unconscious, he may not be able to call out.

A total of 10 people began a systematic search to find Jason. It was now 1:45 p.m. and the Caravan had landed. Bob approached the pilot with the hope that he may have seen Jason making his landing. The pilot never saw Jason come down.

The search continued, and now we also had the pilot helping us. In a situation such as this, looking for your comrade can create the greatest degree of apprehension. Knowing full well that every passing minute can be crucial to the downed individual, only the worst fears fill your heart.

Our search was conducted thoroughly through a 60-acre region of the fields and hills, the trees, two small culverts, and even along several gravel service roads along the drop zone's parameters. No sign of Jason. We had been searching for over an hour and a half, and the time was now approaching 3:30 in the afternoon. We were all feeling knots in our stomachs over the missing man, and finally, Frank, the drop zone owner and manager, had us reconvene in the observation area.

Considering the extent of our search and the lack of results, a decision was made to notify the FAA and a local military air reserve base just 10 miles to our north. The air reserves were great. Within less than a half hour, they had dispatched a helicopter and an additional five-man field team to assist further in our search.

Despite all efforts and continuing the search right up until 7 p.m., no signs could be found of the missing man. The reserves called off any further efforts of the search, and recommended we notify the local police.

Frank declared the drop zone grounded for the remainder of that evening. We had a visit from an official of the FAA as well as the local police, but there was nothing either agency could do. Considering our help from the air reserves, everything that could be done was done. It was suggested that, if we wished, we could continue flying the very next morning. The police would notify members of Jason's family and a missing persons report would be filed.

We all stayed the night with the use of our sleeping bags and camping gear. The beer cooler was hauled out, but moods were sombre.

We slept, and Sunday morning arrived. It was another beautiful day — warm and sunny. Moods were somewhat subdued still, but the cheer began to pick up and by 9 a.m. we were gearing up for more jumps.

By 9:20 a.m., five of us were seated in the Caravan taking off for another exercise in relative work, minus one. Much like the day before, everything went beautifully, yet in only a short while we would each be questioning our own sanity.

We went out the exit, just as before, but this time at 12,000 feet. After the initial stabilization, we went into our manoeuvres. But at approximately 8,000 feet, we ceased all exercises, for no man could believe their eyes, nor any of their senses.

Falling there, right along with us, smiling and waving, was Jason!

It is a thing which I can scarcely relate, the overwhelming shock, the feeling of relief, of puzzlement.

Had we each been victims of a bad joke? Clearly, this must be the case. And though we were all amazed and excited to see Jason falling there along with us, we all had some big questions, and likely some strong words, for Jason.

Naturally, we did no more manoeuvres as we fell through the sky. We began deploying our canopies after 2,600 feet and came down to Earth.

As we each landed and gathered our chutes, I think we each had some idea as to what may have occurred. If this had been a joke, for it most surely must have been, then Jason must have been purposely hiding from us.

Logically, he may have touched down earlier than the rest of us on that first jump, or at least hidden from us, and then likely evaded us as he later hid aboard the Caravan awaiting the next drop. It was possible, that this sour little joke may have involved another aircraft, but there was never any other plane in our airspace at any time of either day. I'm sure we each came to the conclusion that if he were hiding on the Caravan, he could have exited right after us.

But the mystery and madness only deepened, only worsened, for as we landed and gathered our gear, Jason, again, was not among us!

We each approached Bob, who remained the senior man on the field. A variety of thoughts were racing through each man's mind, but I can only say that we all agreed to keep Jason's sighting to ourselves, at least until we could sort out this mystery. I suppose the general consensus was that it was either a bad joke or some form of mass hysteria that the five of us were experiencing. Of myself, I can only say I had the sickest feeling in the pit of my stomach. None of us, it was agreed, would say a word to anyone else outside our circle about seeing Jason.

We stopped by the picnic tables for about 45 minutes, where we took time to repack our chutes and have some coffee. Then, we again loaded up the Caravan and up we went. This time, it was agreed, each man would jump but we would forgo the relative work.

So once again, upon attaining an altitude of 12,000 feet, we each made our dive out the aircraft. There is simply no way to relate what I am now about to say. For unless five men be mad, I say again that we each witnessed Jason in the free fall with us somewhere after we each stabilized above 10,000 feet!

Any sane man would know that this simply could not be. Yet, there he was! Falling with us, though this time, he did not wave as enthusiastically, for he seemed a bit weary and I could see fatigue, and perhaps some degree of worry, in his face. We all called out to him, but he gave no response, he simply shook his head and managed a wry smile.

As we approached the altitude of chute deployment, we were all shouting "pull" to Jason, along with signing an extended index finger — the international parachutists signal to deploy. He didn't seem to respond. We each proceeded to open our chutes, all the while trying to keep an eye on Jason. He sped right passed each of us and simply disappeared.

We landed and gathered our gear. Jason was not with us. Having collected ourselves, yet again, by the picnic tables, we tried to address our mutually shared mystery. We all felt we were very much on the edge. Without drawing any reason of alarm from other people at the jump site who were aware of Jason's disappearance, the five of us decided we would simply not jump for much of the afternoon.

After several hours of consuming hot dogs and coffee, we decided by 4:30 to continue skydiving. At 5:20 p.m. we were back at 12,000 feet diving out, and again by 10,000 feet we found ourselves accompanied by the presence of Jason.

Again and again we jumped. And in each and every case, even though some members sat out the dives and left only two or three of us jumping, we were met with Jason in the free fall period. And yet Jason would never land.

What should go through the mind of someone experiencing such a thing? Were we mad? Could five men be suffering from some form of hysteria? I can only say that we examined and scrutinized our own sanity as best we could.

Should we have reported our bizarre sighting to the others? Should we have notified the police? We never even disclosed to the pilot what we were witnessing. It remained our solemn secret lest anyone think us mad.

On the next and final day of the long weekend, we jumped continually throughout the day. On some flights we had new jumpers and students with us, so we spoke nothing of our mystery. Nor was Jason seen at any time when any other than members of the original five-man team were jumping.

And yet, when any of the original five of us went out alone, there was Jason, forever falling, forever looking weaker and more despondent. And always were we screaming out to him, "pull!"

By the end of that weekend, we all bid each other adieu, and returned to our homes and lives with our bitter secret.

* * *

It has now been some time, and I've returned to Slipstream on only a few occasions, sometimes with members of the original drop team, sometimes by myself, and sometimes in the midst of other skydivers who would never learn or suspect our great secret.

In those cases where I've jumped alone, or with my peers, always did I see poor Jason, forever falling, his state now worsened as in slow death. From a distance, I could see death's dull tone to him and a lifelessness in his eyes. He continues falling, even still, as a lifeless body falls.

Winter approaches now. Our five-man free fall team has ceased and I don't keep in touch with the others. Bob and Frank tried phoning me once, but I missed their call and somehow never got in touch with them again.

Strange, it seems. For in so many of my dreams lately, it is me who is falling. I am falling and it is Jason who is waving and calling out to me. "Pull," he keeps shouting, as I speed below 2,000, 1,500, and 1,000 feet. "Pull," I keep hearing him scream to me as I fall, despondent.

The dreams keep coming. And Jason is always there falling with me, screaming frantically out to me.

It is odd, and I suppose it must be the change in seasons, but as the dreams continue, I seem to be finding it harder and harder to wake up.

I haven't been back for a long time.

STROBE

I was there the day it came down. It happened in late autumn. It was on one of the cross-country trips I take for business when I am called upon to drive the vastness of our great country for my income's sake. I should have made the trip in June, but things delayed that. So my journey was made in late October, when the reds and oranges become browns and yellows.

The nature of my business is not important, nor are most of the details of that particular excursion. Some background may be prudent though, as I am not so reticent of my personal affairs that I would keep such pertinence of matters to myself.

I am 46 years old at the time I write this, and you need therefore know only that it happened when I was but a few years younger. I've been working most of my life. In fact, from the time I was 16 and booted out of the house by the old man, I had to go to work just to survive. As a result, I never finished high school. It was reality right away; hard and fast.

I was raised in a small midwestern town at a time when baby boomers were in full swing, and supposedly had the greatest chance of building strong futures for themselves. I guess some of us fell through the cracks. I had one baby sister, and two brothers who were somewhere around my age. All I ever remember about us was how we used to fight all the time. I guess it was a reflection of our circumstances. By the time Gerty — my kid sister — started growing up, it was time for me to leave. Around that same time I broke off contact with Brad and Hank. I haven't seen any of them since.

My mother was never what you'd call a strong woman. In fact, she slept all the time and seemed constantly ill. I have no doubt that that is exactly what contributed to making my father the tired and burned-out old soul that I knew him to be.

Frankly, I think the war got to my old man. He never spoke much about it, but when he did, he made damn sure you heard him. I'll never forget the day the news came down about the Bay of Pigs. He damn near went berserk the day Kennedy made his address. "First it was the Nazis," my old man would scream, "and now it's those goddamn commies." Then he'd fly into one of his rages and start beating my mother. We all took our turn with the hits though, and because I was the oldest, I got more than my share. Actually, I first remember him knockin' me down when I was just six years old. That's the first time I remember him hittin' me. It's also the last time I ever cried. Six years old and I never cried again. I'd rather not tell you we got used to his treatment, but then again...

He drank, too. It was all part and parcel of our scene. And I hated him. God, how I hated him. But perhaps I'm getting off track. It was my experience I wanted to talk about, the one from a few years back.

It was late autumn, the end of October. During the latter part of an evening, I had stopped by one of those tourist attractions you sometimes see near secondary highways. This particular one was located near several of the largest cornfields you could ever imagine. I barely remember what the information plaque read anymore. I think it had something to do with Cheyenne or Apache hunting grounds of some 150 years ago.

I had pulled off the highway to rest and grab some coffee out of a Thermos I always carried with me. There were two other vehicles already stopped there; a Ford Aerostar and a Taurus Sable. By the time I had pulled in, there were five of us standing outside overlooking the cornfields and reading the plaque. All in all, it wasn't a half bad evening. The sky was clear and there was only a slight breeze. The temperature was tolerable with just a light jacket.

I guess because it was a secondary highway — and in the middle of the week — the road was quite deserted: just a few travellers taking a moment to rest and stretch their legs. The five of us actually made small talk together; strangers in the middle of nowhere enjoying the bond of the moment, without any nervous apprehensions. Some parts of the country are more suitable to this than others.

Collectively, we'd all been there for less than half an hour. And that's when it happened.

I might say it was like a bit of a surrealistic dream, as if we'd all stepped into another world, or another state of mind. It started with a whir that seemed to emanate from the cornfields. You couldn't tell where it was coming from. It was a sound, a sound like nothing I've ever heard; like the low throb of a bass drum with the high pitch of an electric appliance. It came from everywhere — and nowhere. We were all transfixed. At first we all wondered aloud what it might be, but then the strangest melancholy fell over the group. We all fell silent and just stared into the heavens, listening.

After my dad got back from the war, life must have changed hard and fast. He married my mother shortly after arriving home, and took what work he could find. I know he moved a lot from job to job. Finally, he landed work at one of the big steel mills. He was probably lucky he got that job. They kept him on till he retired with emphysema and heart problems back in '72. He died in '76.

It was 1949 when I came along; the first of four. I can't say whether or not they planned on having a family, but it happened. Brad and Hank followed shortly afterward. Gerty showed up in late '62. Oddly enough, it was during those early years that I understand dad started taking to the bottle. He's lucky he hid the habit from the job, or perhaps they knew about it and just let it slide.

He was missing two fingers on his left hand, too. You might have thought it was from some accident in the plant, but in fact it happened during the war, on the beaches. That's right, he was there — on the day. Big D. Half a day's battle into it and he got caught in a hose down with a sniper. The German pegged his left hand before the old man returned fire and blasted the shooter into kingdom come.

But the old man survived. So few did. Living through the war never stopped him from being an absolute grouch though. If I've ever known a bitter and angry man, my father was it. I guess he just never counted his lucky stars by the fact he even came home alive.

The cornfields. We all stood gazing, and perhaps entranced — even hypnotized — by the drone. The sound was like a crescendo, building to some unforeseeable climax. We waited, we listened, and then the fields were ablaze.

It was as if the moon (and there was only a partial moon that evening) had grown to a brilliant deep orange and expanded its light to a point where all the fields were awash with the glow. An artificial light? Perhaps. Yet it appeared to be true light, such as a much smaller sun might exhibit. The sound intensified. And then it was there.

It came down, spinning ever so slowly, huge and magnificent, breathtakingly beautiful, and so mysterious. We gasped and exclaimed. We were transfixed; caught up in another, timeless reality. What was it? I didn't know then. I would never even hazard a guess now. At one moment, it seemed to be the size of a battleship fallen from the skies. Yet, in the next moment you would have thought it no larger than your fist. It was spherical and it appeared solid. And though this may sound odd, I can only relay that intuitively, it did not seem man-made; and was not of this Earth. Stranger still, though it seemed to emit that brilliant light, we could see no lights or portholes which might have been responsible for the glow.

It spun round and round, ever so slowly, in elevated grace. Everything else around us seemed to wither to nothingness. Nothing else was important. We were alone with it. We stood, watching, listening, lost in our mysterious reverie.

He took us fishing once, the old man. I can't say I remember where, but it was somewhere up north near the border. I was 11, so Brad and Hank would have been nine and 10 respectively. It was a very happy time. Just us four guys out doing guy stuff. In fact, I even remember when we were out in the middle of the lake and Hank got a hook stuck in his thumb. He started whooping and hollering like a banshee, but for some reason the rest of us just found it so darn funny that pretty soon we were all laughing and screaming like a bunch of hooligans. Hank survived, however, and after three days we all came back with a trunk full of mackerel. We were like kings back then. The fish stories went on for months.

It's a shame there weren't more happy times like that. I really don't know why there weren't. He started teaching me how to ride a bicycle when I was seven, but he never saw it through with me. I made it though, he got me going and I continued on my own and with the help of other kids on the block. It took me a while, but I learnt how to ride.

Then there was a day when he came home with

flowers for my mother and gave them to her with a big hug. It must have been an occasion or something important to them. I don't know. I was too young to remember much more about it, but it's funny how it stands out in my mind. I'd never seen her so happy. I just keep wondering why there couldn't have been more of those memories.

The strobe twisted and turned like a giant top in the air, keeping us mesmerized. You could swear it pulsated, but it stayed fixed for the longest time in the air. I don't know if it hung 100 feet or a 1,000 yards above ground level: I can't recall a cloud line to compare its elevation too. But it was so beautiful; just hanging there, pulsating, droning on, with the light covering the fields. It lasted for, what? Five minutes? Twenty minutes? We were all hypnotized, fascinated. Then, it started to descend and the droning grew louder.

It was at this point that I remember my head starting to ache. I have no idea what the others were feeling. In a moment the pain became so intense I must have been experiencing a migraine. The strobe lowered itself nearer and nearer the ground, with that dreadful noise reverberating through my mind. It was spinning faster, and the light became absolutely intense. You might wonder why we didn't run and try to locate the authorities. But we were transfixed, see? It held us firm by some unseen force.

Did I black out? I don't know. All I remember was being there, with him.

The beach is completely torn up. Men's bodies lay all around us, many are still alive and screaming in their agonies. Shells are flying overhead and exploding everywhere. Machine gun bursts and gun fire continue endlessly. I've never felt such fear. This is chaos; complete pandemonium. How could so many men go forward to face death? Suddenly, I'm aware of rifle fire, and a round comes speeding by my left ear — his left ear. Thank God it misses. Panic sets in. We drop. Another round explodes in front of us — right in front of us, kicking up dirt! We scream! There's blood! That's the round, the one that takes his fingers. Christ! The old guy's a tough buzzard, he takes the pain — just takes it. He returns the fire. Again and again. He's up. Now he runs forward unloading his weapon and tears into the dirt, still in pain, bleeding. No return fire. He fires again and runs forward — nothing. He got the sonofabitch! Nailed him. But now I see confusion. He's here, the old man is here by the body of the German, the one who took his fingers and tried to kill him. There's something he doesn't understand, something he doesn't want to know. Then the old man falls to his knees, and quietly goes insane.

It all comes loose. The old man is sitting here, crouched on his knees and he's holding the dead German. He's crying, he's crying until he's screaming. He shot a kid! God almighty. My old man killed a kid, pushed into the front lines to defend Hitler's dying, insane dream. The old man screams and screams until he can't scream anymore. He never went to war to kill children. He never even wanted the damn war. All the old man ever knew was peace. All he ever wanted was his own family, his own children. Goddamn this. Something snaps in him. He lives but he is no longer fighting the war. He is out of it. The tears spill onto his uniform and he falls over into the sand and the mud. He is a casualty of war, but not from a bullet. His soul has been broken.

All that follows is blackness.

How long has it been? Minutes? Hours? I'm lying on the ground and a gentle rain is falling, though I don't remember there being any clouds. I slowly start to rise. Then, I remember, didn't I have a headache? But there is no pain. Now there is something else. Something I haven't known for a very, very long time. My eyes are filled with water, though not from the rain. There is another feeling, one that I can't quite explain. Something has been lifted from me. A burden. It is no longer there, just this feeling of lightness. I can't describe it.

I look around and see the others, gradually standing but in slow motion. Now it comes to me. What were we watching? What did we witness? The others, like me, look around and gaze upward. There is nothing. There is no unusual sound, no strange light, and nothing hanging from the heavens; just a gentle rain. The strobe has vanished.

I walk over to my car feeling perplexed. A strange and powerful sensation has touched me. I watch the others move to their vehicles, two are crying, a third seems happy, another just looks so much at peace.

I get in and start the engine. It has been a strange evening. I look at myself in the rear-view mirror and see a very different me looking back; it is the same face, but it has changed. I reach for a tissue and wipe my eyes.

How could I have known? I knew the story. He told me himself, though not all of it. What he didn't tell me was what broke him in half; destroyed him, left him with a questionable future to build from a shattering experience. He was no killer. But then he came face to face with the war, and a mere child thrown into a German uniform to face the same craziness. The kid died on a dirty sand bank. My father was left to wander through life with a wound that would never heal.

I leave the experience and the cornfields behind me in my rear-view mirror. My soul is awash with a feeling I've never known. My eyes are wet. An incredible thing has happened here tonight. And there are three things that I might say I know:

This is the first time I've cried since I was six. No one will ever know what that strobe was, and...

I loved my father.

THE MIND MUST TRAVEL

(or, The Aliens Who Stole My Brain)

Our cosmic brethren — the Mentors — had been in established contact with the people of Earth for 10 years now.

And despite all those sci-fi novels, movies, comic books, and other speculative writings about contact with other intelligent life forms, none had ever really considered just how difficult communication could be with a completely different and unknown race to man's. Most meanderings by fiction writers and film makers had us speaking in fluent English by the same week of first contact.

But in reality, the truth about communication with a new, intelligent, and alien life form proved to be incredibly difficult and challenging. There were, to put it simply, no common bases for communication. Biologic origins were completely different, thought processes were different, senses were different; emotional responses, intellects, and even the way two separate races viewed the cosmos were different.

Fortunately however, there were common grounds through most of the sciences, such as mathematics and physics — and these proved to be the starting point for the establishment of a communicating basis with man and the Mentors.

"Mentors" was a name tossed around by the media back at the beginning of the first contact, mainly because they were superior where the sciences were concerned and would therefore become man's friends, teachers and mentors in these areas. The name stuck, regardless of what they actually called themselves.

Their method of speaking was a form of irritating, high-pitched squeaking, much like the sound a mouse or other small animal might make when caught in a trap. With five small eyes, a loose, rubbery purple skin, and no true mouth, they were, indeed, very different from us.

They also had intellects that were based on the absolute. And this was one of the most interesting aspects about them. With very factual, and supremely logical minds, their entire culture and science had been based on cold hard absolutes — the known.

And this was what really differentiated them from mankind — for the Mentors literally had no art, and in the way we understand it, no imaginations! Their entire fields of math, physics, and the sciences were based on that which was discovered and established logically: 'A' proceeded to 'B', which proceeded to 'C', and one plus one equalled two, and so on. Their entire culture was based on this progression of absolute thought and therefore, the absence of imagination.

This was where I came in.

For as communication became more and more established and fluent with these cosmic brethren, I was assigned as cultural emissary to instruct and educate the Mentors in the fields of the arts — that most important and prominent aspect of man's culture, all of which is based on imagination.

I couldn't have asked for a more prestigious, or difficult, task. After all, how does one explain the arts to a race that has no art? And how does one communicate the need to dream and the desire to create to a life form that bases everything on discovery by logical progression? It was clear that my assignment was no small challenge. Music, painting, sculpture, fictional prose, poetry, and so much more are all based on the imagination of man and the desire to create.

Although in the past 10 years the Mentors had definitely sampled and viewed much of mankind's artistic endeavours and creations, I chose as a starting point a kind of show-and-tell as an assortment of music, prose, and the visual arts.

As we proceeded from Mozart to The Who, Van Gogh to Dali, and Hemingway to Marvel Comics, I could see that we were making very little progress. The Mentors were clearly trying to understand, but there were some fundamental differences. Part of the problem was not in any way made easier by a translator which had been developed by the military. The translator itself catered to the Mentors in that it dealt with systems and principles that were based on the progressions of the literal.

What they — I — needed, was an overview.

If I was to educate a completely alien race about mankind's artistic undertakings and the very important concept of imagination, I would have to relate this in a logical and concrete way that they could understand. And it certainly seemed logical to me to begin an introduction to the arts based on how an artist's mind works, even if it were through a rather simplistic, and elementary starting point.

I'll never forget the day I was, as a child, chided by one of my teachers for having a mind that tended to wander. Well, using that experience, it seemed the very explanation that would be understood by a race of thinkers in the absolute.

We proceeded with the translator and began making progress on the point which I was so determined to establish. Yes, there was registration with this concept. We had viewed many of the great works of the ages; listened to a wide selection of the finest recordings by the masters. We had even delved into the pasts and lifestyles of many of mankind's great artists. But there was still the 'why'. That barrier between what was accomplished by the artist and the very process that brought about its conception — the 'reason to be'. In other words, why was an artist an artist? And what within an artist's mind was it that triggered the mind to create art?

"Well," I tried to explain, "the mind must wander, it must explore itself and thoughts of creation within itself."

And then came the great turning point, as I exclaimed, "the mind must travel."

That must have done it. There was a great commotion among the Mentors as they began excitedly squawking and babbling away in their native gobbledygook. Yes, that was it. Here was the concept they could understand.

"The mind must travel." That was it. They could likely appreciate the needs of the mind to move outside itself, to travel, to explore and dream without the physical commitment of the body. That was as literal as the explanation might get. It was our first great step into the realms of imagination.

And through this great revelation, I became quite a hit with the Mentors. As cultural emissary, I had introduced the race to a completely different dimension of the workings of the mind.

And so it was that I was invited as a guest of honour onto one their great starships for what might best be described as a celebratory "joy ride." With permission from my superiors, I was able to accept what was to be a relatively small ride to the outskirts of our own solar system and a visit to some of the more interesting and beautiful moons and planets in Earth's own neighbourhood.

I readied myself for the great journey, which, in fact, would last no more than a few days. Some preparation was made by the Mentors, and for a brief time, they rendered me unconscious for, as it was explained, "an integral part of preparation for the journey."

When I awoke, we were already in flight. We sped around the sun in all its magnificence and glory. After Sol, it was on to Mercury. From Mercury, we then had a look at our own — the blue — planet. We visited the rings of Saturn and took in all their beauty. Next was Jupiter and her moons — fantastic! Everything was breathtaking. And yet, as I adjusted to the feeling of travel and the incredible scenes of these planetary bodies, I must say that I didn't feel quite 'myself'. And though I contributed my odd feelings to this new experience of space flight, something just wasn't right.

As we continued with the wondrous sights, I tried to ignore the fact that even my eyesight and other senses were somehow, not normal. Trying to relax with the situation, I took in the panoramic views of the stars, a look at Haley's comet, the asteroid belt, and more — all the time telling myself that my strange feelings were due to space travel and my new environment.

We finished our little trip, and as fascinating as it was, I was glad to return to Earth.

It was during our entry into Earth's atmosphere that I became more and more alarmed that something was out of the ordinary. Certainly, I rationalized, I would return to feeling my normal, Earth-bound self once we were off the ship and back on Earth's gravitational plane.

It was at the time that we were exiting the great starship that the Mentors popped their infamous question. And although the question came through the translating device, the meaning was clear enough: "Did my mind wish to travel some more before being returned to my body?"

My mind reeled, as I saw, with the use of electrodes, an assortment of ultra-advanced fibre optics, and technologies as yet unknown to man, that my body — with its head split open revealing a wide, empty cavity — was moved next to the very receptacle that held my brain.

Well, I suppose it serves me right. Somewhere in the translated lingo, words and meanings — for a race that could understand only the very literal — had become very literal indeed.

The mind does indeed like to travel. And I suppose I shouldn't be too upset, after all, the Mentors thought they were doing me a great honour and favour. So much for trying to communicate the arts to a purely scientific race of aliens.

I think it may be time I found myself a new line of work.

MONSTER FOR HIRE

My week had been running rather typically, with few events and even fewer distractions. I left work shortly after five — like always — arrived home about sixish — like always — proceeded to boil my suppertime pasta — and, well, you get the idea.

I can't say that I 'live to work' or even that I 'work to live,' in fact, I like to think I do maintain some sort of balance between most things in my life. And like most people, I have my varied little interests and hobbies that sustain me and provide me with some pleasure and degree of interest outside the workplace.

I also have my own rhythms and time tables in my daily and weekly schedule for the way I do things. For example, I do like to work out and, fortunately for me, the gym I attend is a short 10-minute walk from my rental on Roncesvalles and High Park Boulevard in the High Park area of Toronto. (I might as well inject here that I live in a very ethnic neighbourhood. I'm not ethnic — everyone else is.) But so it is that I like to attend the gym an average of three times per week. Typically, I attend Monday and Wednesday evenings, and if I forgo Friday, you'll definitely find me there on Saturday, working and sweating and finding various new methods of straining and punishing myself amidst a lot of other sweaty and smelly guys who are working and sweating and finding new ways of straining and punishing themselves.

Anyhow, other than a few other outside interests, it is necessary to note that I perform many of my own domestic errands right in my cozy little neighbourhood. The local IGA, for example, is one block away; a variety of small convenience stores run up and down the street; a dry cleaners is next to the IGA; and a laundromat is just two blocks north of me.

And this is really where my story begins.

You see, I do my laundry at this local little coin-operated laundromat an average of twice per week, or perhaps once every five days, depending on my needs. My time spent there usually averages just over an hour, and so, I can conveniently slip in to do my wash during any number of time slots during my busy week.

Well, it was on a Tuesday evening that I was in the process of waiting for a wash load to finish drying that I stood, dopey-eyed, viewing, as one in a state of laundromat boredom views, the bulletin board on the premises.

You've likely had the same experience. I stood placidly scanning the cork board without any real interest, noticing a variety of both hand-written and computer-printed (the latest, these are the nineties, of course) ads for a variety of causes, the most of which seemed to be "Movers for Hire."

Reading the assortment of notices, there were the standard "Nanny Available," "Used Furniture For Sale," and what seemed to be a few too many "Mover Available," and again, "Movers for Hire."

That's when it caught my eye.

In the lower portion of the board, between a

couple of moving notices, read (yes, on laser-printed computer paper)

"Monster for Hire"

And other than containing one very long and strange looking phone number (it had lots of 666's), that was all it said.

Well, I have to admit, I really didn't think much of it. Probably a typo or someone with a rather poor grasp of the English language; perhaps some silly little joke, or even more likely, a teaser of sorts: You dial the number and someone will try to sell you used golf balls or a keg of laundry detergent. No thanks.

I gathered my load of laundry, which had dried by this point, and went home, forgetting entirely about the notice on the cork board.

The following morning came, and Wednesday proceeded along much like any other day in my week. Wednesday evening arrived, as it does toward the end of Wednesday, and I proceeded with my schedule — gym time.

So in I go, prepared for the gruelling workout. Now, I haven't mentioned this as of yet, but it becomes most pertinent to our story's development: Although I am well into my 30s, I have had the most enlightening number of experiences being, shall we say, "intimidated" by one particular individual at the gym. Okay, okay, let's call it by its real name — "bullied," I'm a man in my 30s and yes, I'm being bullied by someone much bigger and stronger than myself.

"Bobby" (Bob?, Robert?, Sir Bob?) is certainly within my age group, though his heavier musculature and shoe-size IQ definitely differentiates him from most nineties men as from the lower protozoa I once studied in high school biology.

Nevertheless, Bobby has on many occasions opted to A) suddenly require the very bench or weights I had been using; B) help load up the bench or leg presses I was situated under with several additional 50 and 100-lb. plates; C) ask me when I'm leaving, what I'm doing here, and do I need a hand out the door; or D) variations on all of the above.

Now, for me not being a man of violence or confrontation, I usually tend to avoid desperate issues as much as possible. I normally insert a bit of humour, and then move on until moods settle down.

Wednesday, however, yielded some rather new dimensions to my existing problem. Bobby — for whatever reason — took it upon himself to get quite vocally abusive with me, and sure enough, one thing led to another until a shoving match ensued. It happens, that although I stand two to three inches taller than Bobby-the-Cretin, he does indeed have a good 40 pounds on me — all of it pure muscle, and I concede, I did finally back down and left the gym in disgust and disgrace.

That night was spent in a rather fitful and seething mood, conjuring up a variety of ways to seek my revenge and blow good ol' Bobby from the face of the

Earth. Fantasy, however, is normally as far as these things go with any of us.

And then a funny thought struck me. Out of nowhere, I remembered that curious little ad stuck to the bulletin board in the laundromat. "Monster For Hire," I believe it read.

I know what you're thinking, just how obsessed can a grown man get over such a silly little episode. Well, desperation is the mother of invention, or intervention — or something to that effect. It's not so much that I thought the note in the laundromat could really lead to anything, it's just that I thought "why not at least make the call, and see where it leads?" After all, if someone on the other end starts trying to sell me used golf balls, what have I lost?

I made my way back to the coin laundry and immediately sought out the notice. It was still there, tacked to the board and I hastened to scribble down the unusually long phone number with all its 666's.

As I walked back home, it did occur to me just how foolish this must be. What was I thinking, that someone was actually advertising monsters for rent? Was it a bodyguard or enforcer type service? Was I going to actually contract some thumb-buster to take care of my little problem from the gym? Could it be some criminal offering their services? All the different notions flew through my mind but I decided I could at least make the phone call, and if nothing else, decline whatever was being offered — including the prospect of used golf balls or the keg of laundry detergent.

I got home and dialled the number.

It rang once only and was answered by someone with a rather raspy, breathy, and heavy voice.

"Monster For Hire," the voice stated.

"Monster For Hire?" I repeated, still rather suspicious and somewhat uncertain.

"Correct," came the reply.

"Well," I continued, "I'm not sure what you're offering, but I have this little problem I need taken care of, and..."

I went on to explain my problem in length. The voice listened and then stated that yes, they do specialize in solving such difficulties, but I would have to come to their office downtown to pursue the matter. They did, the voice emphasized, settle such grievances most promptly. My query as to how much the fee involved left a most curious response.

"You can afford it," I was assured.

"But, what exactly does that mean, I mean, just how much do you..."

"Trust me, you can afford it."

I was given an address and told to be there before midnight that evening — that is, if I was serious about my problem and wanted it solved.

Well, I know what you must be thinking: What fool would go to some business he didn't know, in the middle of the night, to meet the owner of a mysterious voice?

The fact is, I felt quite safe and certain about the

whole matter. Besides, I wasn't told to bring any money, so what reason did I have to get mugged?

I jumped onto the first streetcar that came my way and downtown I went. It took me a while, but having followed the directions I was given over the phone, I found the address I sought: Number 13 — Die'r Straights.

I proceeded into the rather small office building of which I was told to climb the stairs to the top — the 13th floor. Arriving on the main floor of the building, I discovered the elevators were not working, possibly due to security at this late hour, and so I made my way, as originally directed, up the stairs. After getting to the top floor, I continued down the hallway to room 13-A, where I found the door slightly ajar. I entered and found a rather scruffy and not altogether pleasant looking fellow sitting behind a desk. I introduced myself.

"Ah, yes sir, you have indeed arrived at Monster For Hire."

What struck me about the chap were his eyes and the features of his face. The eyes may, in fact, have been clouded by contacts, because they had the most piercing, hazy blue colour. As for the man's features, well, let us just say that he was not a particularly handsome fellow.

We buckled down to business rather promptly, at which time I anticipated and expected some explanations as to just what sort of firm or service Monster For Hire really was.

Well, let me put it this way: You know what a monster is? Right. That's what Monster For Hire employed and promoted — werewolves, ghouls, shadows, hobgoblins, and the like. So how does one conduct a conversation with a monster? Truthfully, I'm still not sure I know.

"Well then, Mr., uh, well what should I call you?" I asked.

"Ernie," came the reply.

"Ernie?" "Ernie! — You want me to call my personal monster for hire 'Ernie'?"

"Correct."

I gave it some thought and decided what the heck, "Okay, fine then, Ernie it is."

"Thank you."

"But tell me," I continued, being somewhat obstinate, "I thought real monsters had long, Latin sounding names that began with 'g' or 'b' or at least 'z'?"

"Well," came the retort, "let me put it this way, if I were to tell you my real name, you might well and likely suffer severe trauma from the fright the name alone could cause you."

("Yeah," I thought, like, give me a break.)

"Okay," I conceded, humouring him more or less, "but there's still at least one outstanding question in my mind."

"Go on."

"Well, so far we've somewhat discussed the contract, but I'm yet to see anything scary about Monster For Hire, or even about you for that matter!"

Well, call me silly but I guess he could hardly resist the challenge. For in the next moment, right before my eyes, Ernie had transformed himself into a hideousness that words could scarce describe, and then almost immediately, yielded himself right back to the very likes of the person with whom I had been conversing from the start.

After picking myself up from the carpet and trying to get a grip on myself and the heart murmur I had just experienced, came the anticipated rhetoric:

"Satisfied?"

"Oh," I responded most enthusiastically, "most satisfied, most satisfied."

"Thank you."

We spoke a bit more at length regarding my concerns and the particular problem of Bobby at my local gym. Ernie assured me that this and any other problems of a personal nature could be easily solved for me, and that I should simply go home to bed and let Monster For Hire do its job.

What I still found distressing was the last detail of business during our short exchange before I walked out the door for that evening. "I'm still most concerned about the one thing you haven't mentioned yet," I said. "Your fee."

"Don't worry," came the reply. "You can afford it".

With that, I let the door close behind me and I was on my way home.

Thursday came and went, and by Friday, I was looking forward to my workout in the gym. All in all,

I have to admit, I thought about Monster For Hire very little the day before, but now that I was on my way back into the gym for my workout, my problem — Bobby — and thoughts of my Wednesday evening meeting all came back to me.

As I entered the gym that Friday evening, I was aware that there was something of a buzz going on between a number of the members. Not giving it any real attention, I proceeded onto some of my warm-ups and finally got into my actual workout. That was when I was approached by Jamie, whom I sometimes shared a bit of idle chat with.

"I guess you've heard about Bobby by now?" he queried.

"Nope," I responded, just slightly suspicious as to where this might be leading.

"Yeah, it seems he was found dead yesterday, apparently from a heart attack. His brother found him in the bedroom of their shared apartment."

(I flushed.)

"Real strange," he continued, "sounds like the poor guy died of fright or something, he was clutching his chest and his face was badly contorted."

Well, that did it for my Friday workout. I finished up and left early, not really sure what my true feelings were regarding this bit of news.

I wandered home and sat for the rest of the evening, pondering this rather bizarre occurrence. Monster For Hire huh? Well, coincidence or otherwise, at least my little problem at the local gym was through with. (Yes, I know, I don't seem overly upset or broken up about the demise of poor Bobby. Oh well, live and learn.)

Not having had any real confirmation as to the how or why of Mr. Bobby's death, I settled down with a favourite book, *Famous Cadavers and Exhumed Remains of the 20th Century,* and gradually fell into a blissful sleep that evening.

The weekend arrived and passed rather placidly, and I did return to a very lengthy and fulfilling workout on Saturday afternoon, all of which I enjoyed without incident.

Then Monday arrived.

Well, most of us have experienced some rather abrupt changes on the job scene, but Monday was definitely the corker. Unbeknownst to me, my manager, Jessica, had been fired late Friday and replaced (already!) with someone quite new to the company — Mike.

Now I should state that Jessica and I always got along royally. We were as two employees should be — a team. We did minimal socializing together, but she was always most helpful and generous to me in all things that mattered.

Suffice it to say, that in the very short space of time of Mike's taking the position as my new manager, I made the unpleasant discovery that Mike was not a very nice guy. Even before lunch of his first day, Mike was down my neck with greater demands for higher sales target achievement, greater administrative responsibility, and in general, a number of other issues which would demand more hours out of my day. These things were going to make my work a great deal harder and my life a whole lot tougher.

I went home Monday night feeling quite exhausted and defeated. I thought, or more hoped perhaps, that Mike would come around and settle in with the rest of the crowd as a decent human being on the job.

No such luck. After several weeks, it just never happened. Mike was a ruthless rogue. And, by coming home so many evenings as exhausted and defeated as I did, I missed most of my precious workouts.

I did take it upon myself to resolve my work disputes and difficulties in a most responsible manner. On at least two separate occasions, Mike and I sat down to have a little 'heart-to-heart' about what I thought had been some of his unreasonable requests, plus, I addressed the issue of his belittling insults which were occurring more and more frequently. Our little chat got me nowhere. I took my grievance right up the ranks, both verbally and in writing — all the way to the top. Still nothing! Mike had been brought in from another company where he had an exceptional performance record for making things happen as a go-getter. Yeah, I thought, but at what cost?

Unable to resolve the issues at hand, I went home one Monday evening and dialled Ernie.

Just as before, the phone rang once only before being answered. "Monster For Hire," came the anticipated greeting. "Ernie," I began, "I trust you may remember me, and I do believe I may be needing your services once again."

So began the process of my, once more, having to make an in-person visit to Ernie's office before the clock struck 12. We discussed matters at length and Ernie again bid me adieu. And, as before, prior to leaving his office, I brought up the issue of compensation for services rendered.

"Well, you needn't worry about it now," Ernie said. "You'll afford it, and besides, that can be tallied up later."

I could have been more suspicious than I was about this unresolved issue of remuneration, but I simply said "Good night," and went home for the evening.

Tuesday morning arrived, and so did a change in the workplace — Mike never showed up.

I proceeded to do my job as a good employee does, and was working quite diligently until about 10 a.m. when the VP Marketing rallied us all together on the sales floor for an announcement. Mike, it seemed, would not be back, since he had the tragic experience of having died that night in his sleep. Or to be more precise, as the explanation went, Mike had actually died 'out of sleep' by what may have well been a heart attack, for his wife discovered him in the wee hours of the morning, on the bathroom floor, clutching his chest and apparently with the most astonished look on his face. "Fright," I recall, was the way the VP Marketing had relayed that astonished look.

Poor old Mike. I returned to my desk and performed

my workday duties with a fresh new inspiration.

Life coasted along in a most rosy fashion for many weeks. My workouts at the gym were frequent, productive, and undisturbed. Work, curiously enough, picked up after Mike's demise, and to date we are still without a replacement for Mike's position. Much of the pressure has subsided. Much is bliss.

There were, of course, a number of incidents where I still felt the need to get in touch with good ol' Ernie at Monster For Hire. There was the manager at my local IGA, where I tend to purchase the majority of my groceries. He just seemed to get more and more belligerent and irksome every time he laid eyes on me. Then there was that pastor from the church up the street who seemed hell bent (excuse the expression) on converting me, being quite sure as he was that I was a very dark soul and was much in need of saving — or persecution — or something like that. Well, he persisted just a little bit too much. I couldn't pass the guy on the street without having him fly into hysterics over me.

Other incidents occurred, such as my encounter with two nasties in the doughnut shop who kept staring at me and then proceeded to get a bit lippy, and that grease-ball biker on the highway who cut me off during one of my Sunday afternoon cruises. But, me being the nice guy I am, I let all those episodes slide. What the heck.

Then too, there was the rude driver of that streetcar I just seemed to be fated to catch every morning on the way to work — and those rotten little kids at the local shopping plaza where I like to spend some of my off time. I guess, when I think about it, there were other incidents after all.

In fact, more and more, people at work, the gym, and elsewhere, seemed to be giving me the oddest little sideways glances. I took to finding it most perturbing and rude. Furthermore, I was continually encountering people who were hostile, aggressive, or otherwise unpleasant. I did think it time to take these issues up with Ernie.

My call to Ernie began as it always did, until I got straight down to business.

"Ernie, my dear old chap, I've got a bit of a question for you."

"Shoot," came Ernie's reply.

"Well," I continued, "it does seem that I've been using your services a very great deal since I first came to you."

"Correct."

"Well," I persisted, "I just can't get it out of my craw that all these episodes are just not in my imagination. I mean, look, I've just been having more and more encounters with troublemakers more than I ever did in my life. Am I crazy, or what? Like, what gives?"

"Well, yes," said Ernie, "that's always the way it does seem to go. It has nothing to do with us really, but it is a given fact that one tends to draw upon themselves that which they would exhibit — and extend the most — to others."

For a moment I was speechless — this needed confirmation.

"Wait a minute," said I, "are you trying to tell me that these incidents have indeed been increasing in number, and that you knew all along that they would?"

"That would be correct," came Ernie's mild reaction.

Again the silence, but I couldn't contain my anger. "You wretch, if that's a thing you had known, it's something you might have warned me about!" I yelled.

"Sorry," said Ernie. "It's not our place to preach principles. You, in fact, came to us for an unspecified but much expected service to be rendered. And I'm sure you would agree, you knew perfectly well — in advance — precisely what services you expected from us. It was much your doing."

I was livid. But then, another thought struck me — what about the debts? I had never made good on any compensation to Monster For Hire.

"But indeed you have," insisted Ernie, "we all create our own debts in life, and are always much our own piper to be paid. I would say that you seem to be paying your debt right now."

He was so smug. There was silence on the phone as I, seething, sought the right words. "That's monstrous," I blared.

"I think, if I were you," retorted Ernie, "I might examine who the real monster is here. You clearly chose not to see our other little notice that always appears right alongside Monster For Hire — it reads, 'Angels For Prayers.' As I indicated," Ernie continued, "one always has a choice in such matters in life. Good night."

And with that, he hung up.

The fiend! The scoundrel! I was betrayed. None of this had been explained to me. How dare he insinuate that I was the monster. How dare he even begin to preach to me anything to do with principles.

I'm not the monster. I'm not the bad guy. All those people who met their ends most certainly deserved it — and maybe then some. But to accuse me? The cad! What game was this? What sly and insidious little plot did he think he was throwing my way? And what was he talking about "angels?" I saw no notice about angels.

I spent my evening sitting and brewing as I had done, so many weeks earlier, seeking a solution to this fiendish betrayal.

There would be justice. There would be retribution. In fact, I think tonight 'round midnight, I'll pay a visit. Yes, I'll pay a visit to Ernie — and not as a client either. Nosiree, tonight it'll be me doing the rounds, and Ernie my dear chap, you're at the top of my list. And perhaps, by morning, you'll even have made the headlines — in a manner to which you may least expect.

And call ***me*** the monster!

PORTHOLE

2206:
J.C. Dorr, 4th Lieutenant, Principal Scribe reporting for the 28th Regiment 2nd Recon Group, Sanction Ops.

This diary is being kept in accordance with current SpecOp observation criteria of the first battalion. This record will attempt to document the occurrences of an eight-man field team from the 2nd Reconnaissance Group — Sanction Operations, and their efforts to locate and neutralize unspecified biologics and other manifestations that may have crossed through the space-time matrix, as originated from the folded space experiments of 2189-92.

The eight-man field team consists of:

Adelson, Sheldon (a.k.a. Shelly or Shel)
1ic/First in Charge
Ali, Ishmael *Secondary Scribe*
Brophy, David C.
Cook,Edwin J. *Principal Medic*
Da Costa, Fernando (a.k.a. Fern)
Dorr, Jon C. (a.k.a. J.C.) *Principal Scribe*
Meehan, Manus (a.k.a. Manly)
SciTech/Secondary Medic
Perry, Robert G. *2ic/Second in Charge*

As befits current SpecOps Diary Methodology, all records herein are written in both 1st and 3rd person, with dialogue of individual team members having been filled in as per observations of Principal Scribe. Should serious injury or death occur to the Principal

Scribe, Secondary Scribe Ali is hereby authorized to continue record maintenance.

This operation began 8/23/2206.

At 0800, the team was dropped into the outer perimeters of the target zone: Old D'Troit. It was here that disturbances were first reported by various intelligence sources: Civvies were reported having been attacked during numerous encounters with bio-logics and other entities. During prep time for this mission, stories continued to surface regarding decimated human carcasses caused by unknown attackers.

The team made its insertion from an altitude of 0600 metres. All went in with weapons at the ready and maintained a degree of high alert from the start of the op.

Upon landing in the designated drop zone, 1ic Adelson briefed the men on the nature of the operation.

"All right," Sheldon began, "we all know what we're here for. Frequent reports have come in from the area of sightings and attacks by unidentified bio-logics. We'll maintain standard scouting positions of single file; two metres between each man; weapons at the ready. Perry!"

"Sir," responded 2ic Robert Perry.

"Get a fix on just how close we are to the nearest known attack site," Sheldon said.

"Checking," came the 2ic's response. Perry was in charge of the grid monitor throughout the op, which could pinpoint to a metre the location of any man in the troop or any portion of the terrain.

"Okay," shouted Perry. "We're close to one of the sites now, less than one kilometre to the northwest."

"Let's go," commanded Sheldon.

We began foot patrol to the sight. Marching through Old D'Troit was like being in a war zone. Ruins from the economic riots of a hundred years previous had never been cleared. Instead, New D'Troit was established to the west, and it was there that many of the communities eventually reestablished themselves. Talk about black and white; night and day. The conjunction of the two cities — new and old — screamed volumes of new hope versus chaos and despair.

We encountered no civilian populations, since this wasn't an area of high habitation. Instead, there were the anticipated transients who lived in squalor and fed on the rat infestations that in turn fed on the transients: the circle of life in an application of self.

Our march hadn't completed the allotted kilometre when the team became aware of a highly putrid and noxious odour. The detestable stench grew stronger as we proceeded, and was definitely not a part of the local filth. As we approached a small rise in the terrain, Perry called out.

"Sir, DNA datsources indicate inanimate altered human remains above the next lift. No life."

"Any toxics, bio-manifests or other dangers?" asked Sheldon.

"Checking," Perry responded. "No sir, just standard ground and air pollutants, not otherwise dangerous."

The way Perry had read out the details from the monitor grid one might have thought he was ordering morning caffeine hits. "Altered human," he had said, and "inanimate" at that. Whatever was lying over the ridge had at one time been human, and either died before or after the DNA alteration.

Each man came to the top of the ridge, and just stared. All your training and previous experiences don't always prepare you for what you may witness in SancOps Recon. No man spoke, but you could see from the expressions that this wasn't going to be your average bug hunt.

Strewn across a 30-metre area would be identified as human remains, that's confirmed, but at first, it's not what anyone might have thought. The whole area was covered with human tissue, pale and pink, as if it had been rolled off some gigantic spindle; laid out like a protoplasmic carpet. There were no specifically identifiable human parts. No faces, eyes, arms or legs, just this grotesque blanket of flesh. And for a while, all the men were fixated on it.

Sheldon barked at Manus to get to work. Manus was the team's resident field scientific-technical officer. If, at any time during an op, elements presented themselves that were foremost of scientific significance, a man like Manus had the authority to counter any order given by the 1ic. Details would then be sorted out by the 1ic and the SciTech man, should the team be considered in peril, or if a significant discovery of scientific merit was viewed as probable.

Manus was busy immediately. Carrying a bergen loaded with scientific field tools, he instantly began pulling out strange assortments of gadgetry that none of the team would ever bother to question. Manus was like a man possessed; poking gauges and wires into the plasmic mass, taking readings, diarizing notes.

During this time, Edwin Cook, the group's medic was also prodding around, making his own assessments. Between the two of them, we could find ourselves studying this find for the next three days, or for that matter, having the op cancelled and being e-vac'd out of the area until more advanced precautions could be implemented.

While the two men studied the mass, the rest of the team just sat, waiting it out until the assessments and the subsequent orders came down.

After several hours, the 2ic, Robert Perry was getting impatient.

"Findings, gentlemen?" Perry queried.

Both men were caught up in their concentration, but after a minute, Manus answered.

"Definitely human," Manus responded. "Impossible to conduct a thorough autopsy right here in the field."

"What can you give us?" asked Perry.

"Quite odd, as you can see," said Manus.

"No kidding."

"Basically," continued Manus, "much like it appears, we're looking at about 400 kilograms of human tissue."

"About the equivalent of seven to eight full-grown adults then?" asked Perry.

"That's correct," responded Manus.

Perry glanced over at the 1ic. Sheldon and Perry just looked at one another for a moment, then Perry persisted:

"Anything else?" he asked.

"Well," cut in Cook, "the mass is lacking bone, but it is possible that the bones have been reintegrated into the overall total."

"Further," continued Cook, "the entire mass is lacking for organism identity, that is, although we know from its volume that this would comprise about seven to eight adults, there is no individual identity remaining."

"It's as if," inserted Manus, "they all went into some gigantic protoplasmic DNA distorting blender, and then got spit out like a single entity."

"Minus the bone," added Cook.

"Well, yes," said Manus, "minus the bone: unless that's in the mix. We just can't tell yet."

Perry thought about this for a while. Sheldon, who had also been taking this in quite intently, now spoke:

"A result of the matrix?" Sheldon asked, referring to the inevitability of the porthole effect we were investigating.

"It would be premature to conclude that now," responded Manus. "However, based on what we're seeing, I think we would have to ask, well, what else could do this? Yes, I believe it must be from the space-time matrix."

"Thank you," responded Sheldon.

Sheldon approached Perry and the two spoke privately. Whatever they were discussing, it wasn't for sharing with the group. After a couple of minutes, Perry came forward and spoke:

"Have you taken samples?"

"That's been done," said Manus.

"Any further work that you can do in the field now," Perry questioned, "or will you want to be giving special orders regarding an e-vac?"

What Perry meant was, would Manus be pulling rank with a SciOp Priority order and deciding what the next step would be for the field team, including the possibility of an evacuation.

"I don't see any reason to red-flag it," responded Manus. "We'll be done and ready to go in a matter of minutes."

Sheldon had been paying close attention to this and nodded. Sheldon would decide the next manoeuvre after all.

Sheldon and Perry conferred again, but this time they were a lot less concerned whether or not they were being overheard. Sheldon had Perry double-check the grid again, checking for areas of previous contact between civvies and God-knows-what. A moment later the order came down: We would march a giant 'S' formation over a 22 kilometre area of the Old D'Troit area. This would be the primary area where the confrontations and attacks had previously occurred. Pending theories of territoriality, even for the unknown biologics, it stood to reason this would still be the best area and plan for extermination.

There really isn't an exact methodology for hunting down entities that may have come through the space-time matrix, considering one doesn't know what is being sought. Anything can slide through the porthole, dangerous or not, living or otherwise, and its origins may never be known.

It's therefore necessary to pursue the entities based on cause and effect of their presence. A team literally has to wait for attacks and other disturbances before tracking can begin. Small arsenals of technology are always implemented to locate the offending intruders, but it still comes down to a high-tech hunt.

Very little is known or understood about the porthole effect. Space-time rips can range in size from that of a man's fist up to the size of a small cloud. Few people have actually seen the rips themselves; they tend to form at random locations within the general area of the original test fields, and then disappear again. These disturbances are thought to take place anywhere from seconds to hours, and it's during this time that the unwanted trespassers pass through.

The entities can be anything, from unknown species of insects, to pollen, dust, microbes, and right up to larger bipeds and whatnot. Sending in special operations teams is actually a band-aid solution to a catastrophe of unknown dimensions. While the team searches for and destroys the biologics, scientists and politicians back in Salt Lake pray that some new deadly virus or bacteria isn't crossing through the matrix as well. It's a concern that's crossed all our minds, but that's the risk factor one faces when agreeing to join the teams.

As for solutions to existing portholes and the problems they create, that's up to the science teams who created the problem. It's a question why the areas aren't nuked. It may be possible that splitting atoms near or through an existing porthole could have far reaching consequences. This may be the reason why the decision has never been made.

Rumours have also run rampant that the portholes were part of the calculated risk of the experiments. This may be one of the reasons why the now-defunct experiments were done in populated areas, especially those consisting of a high number of transients. Such a scenario would be typical of higher powers in their ongoing search for new weaponry, whether biological or physical. And that's a frightening thought, because there are those who believe that whatever is expected to pass through the matrix is something we still haven't seen yet.

The team organized themselves into single file, and began the march. Twenty minutes into it we were being hit by one of the cloudbursts from the heavy pollution. Such rains don't tend to last long. This one was over within less than 10 minutes.

Since we weren't in an actual battle zone, formations were lenient with the exception of the single-file march. A point man, for example, wasn't necessary for the purpose of spotting or drawing enemy fire. If we encountered the biologics we were hunting, they could appear from any direction. More than likely, they would be found through attacks elsewhere in the area.

Perry kept his vigil on the monitor. The grid would show heavy populations to the west, as well as scattered life readings throughout the area. All he could really watch for would be something out of the ordinary; energies appearing out of nowhere; fluctuating or out-of-norm physical temperature readings; or clashes between energies, which would likely signify the attacks that brought us out here in the first place.

The march brought us into contact with a number of transies looking for food and hand-outs. Although the practice is frowned on by the regiment, Sheldon had us pass out small portions of ready-to-eat meals. After over 200 years, army food was still as lousy and unevolved as ever, so few of the men really minded.

Two hours into the march, we had our first call. Reports came in of a disturbance three kilometres to the southeast. Perry tried to confirm this on the monitor, but there was nothing to see. The team back-tracked somewhat and went straight to the reported coordinates. It was about to be our first contact with a biologic.

By the time we arrived, the area was complete pandemonium. About a dozen people were running around screaming. Sheldon began shouting orders as the team arrived on the scene.

"Fan out, all of you," Sheldon hollered. "Let's find out what the hell is going on!"

Every man had his weapon ready. Despite some fog in the area, it was still mid-day, so at least we didn't have to worry about our nightscopes. One of the men's voices rose sharply over the noise.

"Over here, captain!"

It was Cook, who apparently found a wounded civvie. It would be the first of several. Sheldon and Perry ran up together. Cook was standing over a young woman crouched over in the mud.

"Jesus," exclaimed Sheldon, "is she alive?"

"Just barely," responded Cook. "She's in deep shock."

The woman couldn't have been more than 20. As I moved forward, I understood the captain's reaction, she was covered in blood, and it looked like her legs had been fed through a meat grinder. There would be very little Cook would be able to do for her.

"How long since the attack?" Perry queried.

"What ever hit her is what's in this area now!" Cook exclaimed, "this attack is less than 10 minutes old."

Just then, one of the enlisteds, David Brophy, hollered over the mayhem to the 1ic:

"Captain," screamed Brophy, "I've got it over here, it's out of its mind rabid, crazy, or somethin'!"

"Well," hollered back Sheldon, "neutralize the goddam thing!"

By this time, Ishmael Ali had run up to Brophy and the two men opened fire simultaneously on the biologic with the grenade-pistols from their Howazers. After a series of blasts and a few screams from excited civvies, whatever was causing the excitement lay dead. Every man on the team, with the exception of Cook, ran up for a closer look.

Whatever it was, it had certainly expired: quasi reptilian, 35 to 40 kilograms total body weight, strong rear legs and a large massive head with rows of serrated blade-like teeth. Most of the team were interested, but frankly, it was a small matter compared to what we had seen hours ago to the northwest.

Sheldon asked Manus if he wanted to take his requisite samples. Manus was busy in no time taking readings and getting hologram impressions that could be replayed later. The team's next priority would be to care for the people in the area, taking into account that there might be other attack victims or those suffering from shock. Fortunately, there weren't many other injuries, and nothing as serious as the first individual we had seen. Regrettably, Cook had been unable to help that young woman and she died of cardiac arrest from her severe trauma.

Next came the period of questioning those civvies who were prepared to talk to us and help our cause. For the most part, the questions were obvious: Had anybody seen anything out of the ordinary? If so, what and when? Any other contacts? Any peculiar 'weather' disturbances? Questions of that sort.

After talking to half a dozen people, it was an old man who caught the team's attention. Sheldon was doing the questioning, and it was clear he didn't like where it was leading.

"So," Sheldon plied patiently, "you've seen something else — like this?" Sheldon was pointing to the dead biologic.

"Ne, ne lek des," responded the old man. "Net des."

The old man spoke with the spoiled English of a generation gone without much human contact, little or no education, and a lifetime built from the spoils of destitution. Sheldon wasn't really having that much difficulty, though, so he persisted.

"Like what?" Sheldon asked.

"Lek, lek, mech ded," said the old man.

"Much dead?" Sheldon repeated.

Manus broke in. "It's possible he may have seen something similar to our earlier findings."

"I realize that," responded Sheldon. Sheldon turned back to the old man and continued. "Where, where did you see these dead?"

The old man didn't speak, he just turned and pointed toward a portion of Old D'Troit that our earlier march would have taken us into anyway. Sheldon now spoke to Perry.

"Look," said Sheldon, "we're not going to base the team's manoeuvres on the probable hallucinations of this transie, but it is possible he may have seen something, and the direction he's pointing is in the area of our original march. Let the team get into their rations, then organize and we'll move out, as before."

We were given a chance to bolt some food and

water down, at which point Perry barked for the team to fall in and we started back into our march. The area we would ultimately enter would take us into a densely populated region of Old D'Troit. The old man may have actually seen something; we would just have to wait and see.

We found our way onto our original route and began the tab. It was now approaching 1800 hours, 10 hours since we entered the area. For the most part, it would be getting dark shortly, and the commanding officer would have to decide whether we were to keep up the patrol through the night or if we would be stopping. It wouldn't be uncommon for the 1ic to have us go throughout the entire night and into the next day. The SancOps teams tend to work intensely over short periods to complete their missions. Men in these ranks are used to pushing hard.

By 2030 hours, we were still tabbing with darkness descending. It was beginning to appear that we would continue through most if not the entire night.

At 2100 hours, Shelly had Perry double check the status of the grid monitor which Perry had been watching periodically. We were now approaching the ruins of the city proper. It stood to reason that the captain would want to have a report before we progressed much further. Perry's response was as expected; a heavier source of life-form readings existed further into the ruins, but in the short distance ahead the population thinned out dramatically.

Shelly thought about it for a moment and decided

we would simply proceed. Any stops would be decided as per the route ahead. None of us could have known it, but we were about to make a ghastly discovery.

And we were heading into a war zone.

Several kilometres into the city, the population suddenly became very scarce, just as the monitor had indicated. All along, we had seen more and more transies and civvies. But now that had stopped, and we were in an area where the numbers should have been heavier.

The 1ic's intuition must have been running high: He gave an order for 'heads up' and weapons at the ready. Although it was now dark, we still hadn't switched to our night scopes, preferring to allow our night vision to develop. We came around a long bend in the road and wandered straight onto the scene.

Here was the reason for the monitor's lack of response to life readings: There were people here all right, but they were all dead. Strewn across an area of approximately two square kilometres were about 50 to 60 bodies, now in the process of decay. The stench was terrible. The commander didn't waste any time:

"Manus — Cook!" Shelly ordered, "I want to know NOW if there's any danger to the team from contamination in the area. Scribe!" Shelly now spoke directly to me. "Be sure this gets documented — all of it."

That wasn't necessary, I was already performing my duties. Despite the scene at hand, Sheldon seemed to be more excited and anxious than might have been expected. The team had to anticipate such scenarios, but Sheldon was clearly suffering some angst.

Once again, Manus was going to be the authority in this situation, deciding what action the team would take. He and Cook were immediately busy rolling over bodies and taking tests.

"Okay," Manus said, "again, we don't seem to have any contamination in the area outside the early process of decay of the bodies. This is definitely not viral. No microbe was responsible for this."

"Get your answers to me as quickly as you can," Shelly replied.

"Well, right now," Manus continued, "it's more speculation, but I still feel this is a direct effect from the matrix. Cook and I will confirm as soon as we're able."

Manus starting having other members of the team move and check the bodies. Everyone was busy. In the meantime, Shelly and Perry were having another one of their private conversations.

It wasn't more than 20 minutes that Manus spoke up again, for all the men to hear.

"Captain," Manus began, "we may have some answers."

"Let's hear them," Shelly responded.

"This situation is not unlike what we first encountered earlier in the day: These bodies have been transformed by something, but not biological or chemical."

"Go on," Shelly said.

"Well, in a different form," Manus said, "these bodies have been through something not unlike the protoplasmic mass we saw earlier; they've been altered."

"But not as extensively as what we saw earlier," Perry said, breaking in.

"No," Manus responded, "not that extensively. However, these bodies have been altered. Internally, everything is wrong. They're likely dead because of the rearrangement of the internal parts and the shock caused to each individual."

With this, Shelly and Perry became silent and simply exchanged glances.

Manus and Cook also spoke between themselves, and now, Manus approached the 1ic and Perry.

"Captain," Manus broke in, "I'd like to speak to you, privately, if I may."

Shelley nodded and the two men moved to the side. As Principal Scribe, I have as much right to listen to such conversations, provided I can get away with it. I moved up and joined the two men.

"Captain," Manus started, "we're seeing a pattern here which may never have been documented before from any previous porthole effect."

"Pattern?!" the Captain jumped on the word.

"Sir," Manus said, "we won't have to see any more dead to know that deaths are being caused in the area by some form of DNA quasi protoplasmic scrambler..."

"And?" Shelly was being a bit difficult.

"Captain..." Manus' tone had that condescending quality of someone who was trying to make an obvious point to a very obstinate person.

Perry had approached us and stood on the parameter of the conversation. There was silence as the Captain thought for a minute. Then he spoke to Perry.

"Have the complete team fall in, now," Sheldon said to Perry.

Perry looked quizzically at the Captain. But Sheldon spoke just one more word.

"Proceed," he said.

After the team gathered, Shelly got down to business with his announcement; it was truth time.

"Prior to the team setting out for this op," he began, "geographic/weather disturbances and biological anomalies were reported in this general area and were concluded to have been caused by the space/time porthole matrix phenomena, as created from the folded space experiments of 2189 to '92. Everyone has been clear on this."

There was nothing for the group to respond to — yet.

"What you didn't know..." he continued, "is that this is the second SancOps team sent into the area."

That caught everyone's attention.

"The first eight-man team disappeared," Sheldon said. "It's unknown what happened to the first team, but we may now have some indication."

Sheldon had just dropped his bomb. And, true to so many military career heads, he made his statements without a single trace of emotion. Every man in the group just stared at one another.

"Wait a minute," Manus now said. "Did you say we have 'some indication' of what happened to the first team?"

Sheldon never answered.

Now Ishmael Ali cut in: "Are you telling us that that mess we saw earlier today...", he stopped abruptly.

"Jesus!" Brophy exclaimed.

"Captain..." Cook started.

Manus cut Cook off. "Captain," Manus said, "this morning, you seemed concerned about the mass we discovered — and it's relative weight against the number of adults it would have taken to create it."

"Right." Sheldon answered quite simply.

"Well," Manus continued, "did you suspect — or know — that that was the previous team?!"

Right about now the men were beginning to get a bit restless and verbal. Sheldon snapped at the bunch of us.

"Look," he barked, "everyone just settle down! We didn't know then and we still don't know if that was the first team or not." Sheldon now directed his comments to Manus. "Your DNA tests will tell us that based on the records of those men who went into the field. Until then, we might assume it was the team, but we STILL DON'T KNOW!"

Voices were starting to rise. Everyone was getting unsettled.

"Right now," Sheldon continued, "we'll continue as we have been all along. As far as we know, this HAS been caused by the properties of the matrix. And we're here to put an end to the problem as well as disperse with any dangerous biologics which may have come through."

"Anything else you aren't telling us Captain?" Cook asked sarcastically.

"You are now updated on everything you need to know," Sheldon responded.

"Everything we need to know?" Cook couldn't believe it.

"You know how the military works mister," Perry stated.

And it was true: it always had been true and always would be true. Every man there knew it. Soldiers around the globe and in centuries past only operated on a need-to-know basis. It was a method of security within — and outside — the ranks. Enlisteds, as well as officers, were only informed of those matters which affected the duties they had to perform. Knowing anything more could be dangerous to the security of missions.

It was clear that information was still being held back.

Perry double-checked with Manus and Cook if more studies were needed in the area, which there were. Everyone felt they had plenty to grumble about, but despite that, all the men went to work under the direction of Manus, who had them go over each body looking for physical peculiarities as well as gather samples. This took some time and we weren't finished until 2330 hours. That was when Manus came and spoke to me directly.

"Dorr," he said, "I realize this is going to be out of standard diary methodology, but I want you to make a record of something I have to say directly, brief though it may be."

As part of the team I'm here to make records, so I acknowledged my agreement. With that, Manus continued.

"All the bodies here have been uniformly and consistently altered, as if by plan. These are not just some random deform... or rather, reformations. Each body here has been as precisely altered — biologically — as the next. These observations are documented in my own records and I will now discuss them with the CO. But I still wanted you to have this in your records direct from me. It is my opinion, as SciTech team leader, that we've encountered the aftermath of something other than, or in addition to, the effects of the porthole."

And with that, Manus approached Sheldon and Perry, supposedly to announce what he had just told me. So, what did this mean?

It was odd enough that a man in Manus' position would have made such a statement to the team's scribe. It was also clear he had done so because he didn't trust what the team leader, Sheldon, would do with the information. Perhaps that stood to reason based on what information Sheldon had held back from the team. But it was also very curious: "altered, as if by plan" Manus had told me... "as if by plan."

Manus clearly had the attention of Sheldon and Perry. Perhaps their reactions wouldn't be quite what he was expecting, they seemed to be nodding as if in agreement. In a moment, however, Perry broke off and made an announcement to the group.

"Okay, gentlemen," Perry announced, "we'll be finishing up momentarily. Cook and Manus will be placing incendiary devices over the remains of the bodies to destroy whatever's left and prevent any chance of germ growth. We'll then set off to a point roughly three kilometres to the south and set camp for the night. Looks like we'll all be getting some sleep after all."

Everyone was certainly happy to hear that.

The remains of the bodies were torched and the team proceeded to a point of flat land to the south. Perry still watched over the grid monitor, but nothing came up during our short march. After we established camp, every one was more than eager to dig into their rations and then head for sleep straight away. All in all, it had been a full day.

Before we all buckled down for the night, Sheldon had a few more words for us.

"We'll rise at 0630," Sheldon said. "The monitor will notify us during the night if any weather disturbances or God-knows-what should endanger us here."

The monitor was capable of serving as troop

watchdog and alarm. If anything out of the ordinary occurred anywhere near us, it would start humming like a bee. Sheldon was still referring to the porthole as "weather disturbance," but each man knew exactly what he meant. If in the event it appeared near our area, previous reports and data stated that it may in fact appear as an electrical storm, wind tunnel, tornado, or some other disturbance not common to the area. We would just have to wait and see.

Before falling asleep, I checked the time: it was 0112. Most of us would get barely five hours of sleep.

It was 0426 when I jolted awake. I had slept well until that moment. The others were up immediately too. The alarm on the grid monitor was screeching away and we were surrounded by lightning and high winds. Oddly enough, other than the haze of pollution in the atmosphere, there didn't seem to be any cloud cover: Stars were actually shining through. We were about to have first-hand contact with a space-time rip.

Every man was up in a flash. The winds and lightning were increasing in intensity and seemed to surround us. The alarm was really going crazy, and then it hit.

Brophy was the first to go. He had been struggling to gather his gear and grab his weapon when he suddenly got yanked back and upward violently; then, he was gone. Vanished! It was as if he had been lassoed and pulled through some invisible doorway. He didn't even have time to react.

It was the matrix.

Sheldon and Perry were going crazy, screaming orders, but everything was happening so fast. Ishmael Ali was the next to disappear. Ali was on the opposite side of where Brophy had been standing. Both men had been on the periphery of the group. Ali never knew what was coming, he was standing there one moment, and in the next he blanked away as if somebody had thrown a gigantic invisible blanket over him. If this was the matrix, it was not acting — or appearing — the way we had been led to believe its properties worked.

Now panic started to set in. The two men who vanished had stood on the outside of the group, and were gone without a second to react. It was odd because the disappearances did not seem to be random.

The sounds from the winds and electrical currents were reaching intolerable levels. Sheldon was trying to scream over the noise.

"Heads up, heads up! Perry! What's that monitor telling us? We've just lost two men!"

"Checking, checking," Perry hollered back. "I can't get a reading! It keeps phasing in and out."

"Captain," Manus interrupted. "Brophy was on the periphery of the group and was the first to go! Ali was next, and he too was separate from the rest of us!"

"Hell," screamed Sheldon, "I know that, so what?!"

"Sheldon," Manus persisted, "it wasn't random! If this is the matrix, it had to cut around the rest of us to get at Ali after taking Brophy!"

"Perry!" Sheldon wailed. "Is that thing going to give us anything or not?"

"I can't pinpoint it," Perry responded. "I can't get a read!"

With that, Sheldon screamed out to the group, "We're not going to wait. Everyone! Cut north — NOW!"

It was an attempt to evade whatever we were in the midst of. Every man grabbed his weapon and all that we could get away with, and we started running northward to escape the matrix's storm.

It was every man for himself. A couple of us hadn't gone 50 metres when we heard a muffled half-scream. When we turned, Cook was gone. He had lagged behind, perhaps because he was slow to start, and now it looked like the matrix had swallowed him. We were down to five men.

After a short one-kilometre run, we seemed to have gotten away from the storm, without its following us. That's when Sheldon had us stop.

We were in the midst of some broken-down buildings hundreds of years old. The fact that we had lost three men was now a fact of life. It was hard luck for them, but the rest of us were happy to have gotten away.

Perry went back to the grid monitor again, but his findings were not conclusive. Oddly enough, the monitor hadn't been much use to us when we were right in the middle of the storm. It wasn't able to pinpoint the actual matrix. Fortunately though, its alarm system had awoken us when the disturbance approached.

We listened to the storm from the distance. It was dying out as quickly as it had formed. There wasn't really a lot we could do. The situation was: we were down three men and had just encountered something that must have been the matrix. The men had to be presumed dead, but even that was uncertain. The fact of the matter was that we were here to deal with the matrix and its effects, so it didn't come as a big surprise when Sheldon ordered us back to the same area with the storm having dissipated.

We walked back to the source of the disturbance where the three men disappeared. When we arrived, we were all startled by our discovery, though in retrospect, it was something we could have expected: there, face down, were the dead bodies of the trio who had vanished.

Once again, Manus was busy making his assessments. The rest of us just stood around waiting for the verdict. Sure enough, the men were dead, and just like the bodies we were investigating only hours earlier, they had been altered structurally, though you wouldn't have known it to look at them. This time around, Manus was determined to examine these structural changes more thoroughly. He shared his observations with the entire group.

"Just as before," Manus said, "they've been physically altered, primarily internally, and it doesn't appear like surgical alterations."

"How do you mean?" asked Perry.

"The alterations are biological," Manus responded, "but not in the way that could be done in surgery. These bodies have been reformatted, changed, but not by laser scalpel or biomed-technology."

"You mean," Sheldon cut in, "not by a medical technology that we are familiar with, don't you?"

Everyone just stared at Sheldon, but he continued. "Look, I want to be on the same level playing field as the rest of you. Any team commander has only so much information: as much as he and his team may need to complete an operation, right?"

"Fair enough," responded Manus.

"I can't tell you what's happening out here because I don't know," said Sheldon, "but I can tell you that I've been formulating a few hypotheses of my own."

We'd just lost three men and I guess the captain felt that now was as good a time as any to start sorting out any mysteries. It was obvious he had been developing his own theories. Sheldon went right into it.

"I know you've all seen me confide with the 2ic in privacy during this mission. Other than what I relayed to you earlier about the first SpecOps team in this area, I'm as much in the dark as the rest of you about all this, but I think I'm starting to see a bigger picture and the 2ic concurs with my opinion, right Perry?"

"Correct," responded Perry.

"Fine," said Sheldon. "Then let me detail my observations and theories right now."

Then Da Costa cut in, "Sir, what if the matrix reappears?"

"And that it may," said Sheldon. "Keep the monitor scanning and our eyes and ears perked-up ladies, we're down three men and this is as good a time as any to figure out what's going on."

Sheldon went straight ahead. "When these porthole effects began, there'd been plenty of reported weather anomalies right from the start. After a while, biologics started slipping through, but that in itself was always, and still is, a bigger question of other ramifications. For instance, have the biologics been slipping through from another time? If so, past or future? But then we get into the question of whose past or future? Is it a different physical plane connected with Earth? Must be, at least that's what they tell each of the special operations commanders before they go into the field and perhaps get slaughtered themselves. But you see, one of the interesting things about the portholes is the very fact that originally, nothing was coming through; they were just storms. Then, despite some of the storms becoming minimal risks themselves, we had small, resilient little beasties coming through the damn rips."

At this point there were some chuckles, but I noted that Manus had the groan of a man who long ago arrived at the very point the captain was trying to make.

Sheldon continued. "So, in addition to the small and irregular biologics coming across, we had the development of a more sordid type. In other words, there was development in the type of entities coming through the matrix. Now, first of all, we might wonder how these things are being sucked up at all from the 'other side' of the matrix. It's more than curious that anything might come through. Think of it: The chances of some alien or other world biped being swept up and sucked into a weather disturbance — like a tornado — can and might happen, but the frequency of this occurrance is hard to accept as a natural process in the case of the matrix."

More nods of understanding from the four of us listening. Manus was gazing at the captain, waiting for the inevitable conclusion.

"... and one more significant point: Each time the matrix reappears to us in its storm-like form, something happens. Either a biologic passes through, or God-knows, people are being sucked into it, and we've all seen the results of that. Such results, I might add, are something of a recent development."

"You think the matrix is being controlled," Manus said it like he was making a statement.

"I don't know," responded Sheldon, "but yes that's what I think, and Perry here agrees with me. The problem is, I don't think the matrix is being controlled from here."

"Here?" queried Da Costa.

"Earth, you know." Sheldon paused for a moment. "It seems damn likely that some other intelligence on the other side has control of the space-time rip, and that should scare the livin' hell out of anybody if what you've seen hasn't scared you enough already."

"Is that possible?" asked Da Costa, "I mean, isn't that a bit remarkable?"

"No, it's exactly what I've been considering." Manus responded. "There's no other way to explain the precision and control of the matrix, or its effects. Look at the way we just lost three men."

"That's right," said Sheldon. "Look at it this way: Years ago the space-time matrix is formed and it connects — what? Two or more different worlds? Two or more different times? Even two or more different realities! On this end we think we're dealing with a batched job in cosmology and physics, but those biologics sent through may have been sent like trial entries from the other side."

"In the same way they used to send dogs and monkeys up in the early attempts at space flight," interjected Manus.

"Correct," continued Sheldon, "and from there 'they' or whatever, begin to advance their own experiments."

"And who or what are they?" asked Da Costa.

"God only knows," said Perry.

"And we may never want to find out," said Sheldon. "Nothing of what we've seen looks like the friendly 'hello' message we might hope for from another race, alien to our own. But then, we have to keep in mind that if we are dealing with a completely different intelligent life form and culture, they may not have any idea or concern about the possible effects from their side — that is from their view point — of the matrix."

"This could be contact!" exclaimed Manus, now realizing the many implications of what could be transpiring.

"Yes," said Sheldon, "this could be THE contact that man has dreamt about for hundreds of years, and if so, it's likely not happening the way anyone might ever have imagined."

"What I'm not clear on," said Perry, "is why 'they' if there is another intelligence on the other side, is committing acts that are clearly aggressive and destructive. Surely a more intelligent, or equally advanced race as our own, would be more conscientious about bridging the gap or making contact."

"No," said Sheldon, "that's wrong and jaded thinking. You're thinking like a human being who knows and has only known one planet, one planetary ecosystem, one sentient race. From their point of view, if they are even aware of us being intelligent, they may no more respect our intelligences or our life anymore than we've ever respected the intelligence and culture of rats. The people they've gotten hold of and altered may actually be nothing more to them than the equivalent of THEIR rats. Think of that! On the other hand, they may be as far removed from our thought processes — or methods of communication — as we are from the octopus. Communication could be near impossible between two such races. Try explaining twentieth-century water colouring techniques to a blind sea crustacean, and you'll begin to understand some of the potential problems. If there is something on the other side, for all we know they're from a distant future, or very different past — and reality."

"But then we would have to conclude that they're non-friendly," said Perry.

"Hell," continued Sheldon, "I'm prepared to make that conclusion anyway. As commander of this op it's up to me to decide what action we'll take. And I'm definitely not on the side of waiting for some unearthly intelligence to come pokin' its nose through the matrix to say 'Hello' to the good people of Earth. For cryin' out loud, look at the results so far! Other worldly cultures be damned, the results of contacts have all been destructive. The fact is, gentlemen, something may already be in the process of trying to get through, and any time that happens, people die. What's worse, whatever the hell is on the other side is likely learning more and more about us with each and every contact. I'm of a mind that it may be time to close the matrix once and for all."

During this time, we had been somewhat fortunate because the matrix did not reappear, though some winds and rain had continued in the area. Sheldon wanted to be sure that the grid monitor was being well utilized, but Perry couldn't find any sign of more disturbances.

We had to get down to brass tacks. The assessments

by the CO had been made, but now we had to make some serious decisions. Everyman understood that we were out here to destroy invading biologics and halt any potential problems that might be caused by the effects of the porthole. I think we all had a fairly good idea where this was all heading.

The commander was likely already making the decision to nuke the area in an attempt to seize and close the space-time rips. He had the authority to do so, no one would questioned that. But what could that mean? If we were on the eve of contact with another intelligent life form, the opportunities we might be giving up could easily out-weigh any consequences for allowing the contact to happen. It was one of those matters better left to philosophers and politicians. The hard and cruel truth was that we might be leaving the door wide open to hostile invading forces. And this was the military: to serve and protect.

Sheldon moved away from the group and got on to SatCom to relay the past day's activities and his observations to Salt Lake and SpecOps HQ. He was in a quandary and wanted advice. If he did consider nuking the area, it would wipe out hundreds, even thousands of people, unless we were prepared to undertake a thorough e-vac of both transies and civvies in the entire area. We were here to help, not commit mass murder.

Sheldon couldn't have been on communications for more than two minutes when the monitor started going haywire. It seemed that the matrix was making a reappearance in the original area of the storm from just a few hours previous.

"Captain!" shouted Perry. "We're live again!"

Sheldon signed off SatCom and ran up to the rest of us. You could hear the winds picking up and the crackle of a heavy electrical storm.

"The matrix again?" Sheldon asked.

"The scope is going wild," said Perry. "Take a look at this, the energy developing is astonishing!"

"What does it say?" asked Manus.

"It's showing electrical envelopes beyond anything we've seen!" blurted Perry.

"Sir!" blurted Manus. "No records regarding this phenomena have come anywhere near energy readings like this. It's well beyond anything we know."

"Do you advise moving..." Sheldon barely got the words out before Perry cut him off.

"TOO LATE!" Perry screamed.

It was almost instantaneous. The moment Perry screamed, the storm cut open with a deafening crack. In that same moment we were all peering at some sort of gaseous cloud that looked like a huge wind tunnel, but it seemed to spin without causing the typical chaos that should have accompanied it. A rip! And yet something from beyond was present. Every man there must have felt it; something was coming through.

And one thing I knew for certain, Sheldon was right: people were going to die.

* * *

Principal Scribe's Personal Log: 9/19/2206

It's a shame what happened that day: Mission date 8/24/2206.

Da Costa, Manus, Perry and Sheldon all perished: Missing In Action, Presumed Dead. Their bodies have yet to be found. I was lucky though, the sole survivor from yet the second SancOps team sent in to source out the dangers of the matrix.

I say it's a shame because I was really starting to like those guys, especially Sheldon. He had a great deal more savvy than he let on, right up until the end. Odd though, for a person as smart as he was, how he didn't seem to pick up on how the storm reappeared as soon as he disclosed his assessments — and his intentions — to the group.

It was clear he wanted to destroy the matrix. And he would have done it, too. But then, that would have ruined it, ruined it for them, the others, the Old Ones. Then they wouldn't have been able to continue their transgressions across the matrix, or plan for their time of crossing. And that would have delayed things, delayed what is ultimately destined to occur: the domination and slavery of the human race.

Everything worked out okay though, I did my job like a man of reconnaissance sets out to do. And those men? Oh, they're dead all right, and they didn't die quickly or easily either, not considering all the things the Old Ones would have to subject them to in order to learn about the human race.

Funny thing, too. I've just been notified that I'm to make preparations as Principal Scribe for yet another team planning an operation for the matrix. Well, that's okay, in fact, I wonder if Sheldon ever figured out in the end that I was Principal Scribe for the first team as well. Probably not, after all, it was all conveniently classified information.

And of this new team, I might say I wish them well. But then, I know better. I know a lot better.

And there are those, I dare say, who know better still.

IVORY ANGEL

Are we to believe in angels? Perhaps if we are to admit that they appear in a number of forms and assist us in a variety of ways, then I must find myself a believer, for I am alive today thanks to one very special little angel in particular.

Some time ago, toward the end of summer, I went tripping downtown on a Sunday afternoon to visit a favourite drug store. Perhaps it was just an excuse to get out for a bit, because I also used the trip as a reason to stop for some brunch at one of my preferred restaurants. It was, as they say, a lazy day, and in truth I am not far from the downtown core, so the trip was less than half an hour by streetcar and subway.

Life in big cities can be tough — there is certainly no great revelation to that statement. In an eastern city with a population of four million, which can swell to seven million during the summer months, there is always that element of human carnage — the homeless and desperate found begging on the streets of our cities in the nineties.

It is something I see often. Since I travel within the city primarily by subway, I am frequently put upon by those less fortunate, who are forced to sleep and wander within our subway systems and on our streets. It is a situation which I find deplorable, for I believe that no person should have to face such desperate means.

And though I have not the makings of a saint, I am not without some degree of philanthropic disposition. This I say because I rarely refuse a street person help, should they ask for a handout. In fact, I typically make it a habit to carry a number of two-dollar coins to pass out when I am able. (Though this may sound somewhat meagre, I should point out that I am by no means well off, and with the number of people asking, two-dollar coins are what I am best able to give.)

It was on this particular Sunday, after having enjoyed my meal and completed my shopping, that I returned to one of the main subway entrances to begin my journey home. As I descended the stairs, I passed a young man crouched on the ground, who very politely asked if I had any change. Realizing the request was in earnest, I drew a two-dollar coin, passed it to him, and continued down the stairs.

It was then, arrested by his call of "wait!" that I stopped and turned to face him. He had his arms out, extended, and was motioning that he had something to give me. As I walked back toward him, I could see he had a number of the most curious little figurines sitting before him, and wrappers of Ivory soap pushed to one side.

"Thank you," he exclaimed, "I want you to have this, I made it myself!"

As I approached and took the item, I could see that it was a small angel, not two inches high, that he had carved from a bar of soap.

"That's incredible," I said. "Did you actually carve this yourself?"

"Yeah, I hate to just beg, so I do all my own carvings out of soap."

"That's truly incredible," I stated, and meant it. His carvings were marvellous.

"Yours is an angel," he said, becoming very animated. "It'll keep you safe."

I thanked him again and pressed on. As I continued down the stairs, his last words to me echoed down the corridor.

"God bless you, sir."

The little soap angel truly was amazing. It was snow white in colour and full of detail. I studied it as I rode the subway to my streetcar connection.

When I finally arrived home, I sat the angel down beside my phone where I would see it every day. It occurred to me that it was both wonderful and, yet, at the same time, sad that someone so kind and talented could be so needy. That stranger's little soap angel graced the two-storey condominium I rented in the city's west end.

I told just a couple of people about my little ivory angel, and indeed, it did remain very special to me. Oddly enough, though I frequented that very same subway entrance during my commuting work week, I never again saw the young man who had given it to me along with his blessing.

It was weeks later, in mid-October, that my dreadful experience occurred. It is that type of experience which we all read about in the daily newspapers, and yet hope — or assume — will never happen to us. But I was, to some degree, lucky, or perchance, blessed.

For as I slept in the second floor of my apartment

during the wee hours of Oct. 14, I was startled awake by sounds coming from the floor below me. The sounds were not loud, and though I sleep very deeply during the darker months, it was the kind of sound that would jar one awake. This I say because I live alone, and as we all know some sounds are alien to our homes, and therefore to our subconscious ear.

Now, although I can say I've been around and I'm no fool, I nonetheless took it upon myself to venture down the stairs and investigate from whence the sounds came. This I did from the inner knowledge that an intrusion — a crime! — was possibly being perpetrated upon my home and, thus, upon my person. An anger wells within one when the realization hits that doing nothing is in itself inexcusable.

Down the stairs I went. The lights were off and it was dark. The lower floor suddenly seemed ominously quiet, and I knew it had not been entirely by my imagination that I found myself wanting to investigate. I reached for the lights, and 'click!' — on came the overhead track lights.

And there stood the intruder. Wearing dark clothing and with tension etched deep into his cold, ruddy face: He was tall and held a flashlight in one hand, and in the other hand a gun! — aimed directly at my chest.

"You should have stayed out o' this," he declared, with some tension but with little remorse.

"And you," I responded, "are better off starving, sleeping in a dumpster, and living the life you deserve, rather than stealing from those who work for their goods."

It was cheeky and a foolish thing to say under the circumstances, but how can I explain my anger at the feeling of this violation? I had spoken quickly and from the heart, without thinking through the ramifications to my sharp tongue.

We stood six feet apart, directly in front of one another. The tension was thick and the moments seemed to extend. I knew not what to do. The gun was levelled at me, and the intruder's eyes showed no degree of compunction about using it.

What was I to do? Trying to rush the intruder would have spelled my end. We gazed intently at one another, neither of us knowing how now to proceed.

And then, his eyes changed and it seemed that there was a fit of anger welling within him. He raised the weapon to my eye level, and I knew I would likely be the recipient of his bullet! I would die with my instincts for confronting this criminal in the intrusion of my home. Such a pitiful end for nothing.

Then! In as much in the same moment as he was about to pull the trigger, my would-be assailant's eyes became wide, and his face seized up! Before I knew it, he had dropped both the flashlight and the gun and was now down on his knees gasping for breath and clutching his throat! It was clear that he was choking, though I knew better than to approach him.

Soon, he was lying on his side, and his face had turned blue — the man was dying before my eyes!

Yet, I remained where I was and did not try to help. As he gasped and sputtered a final breath, there he lay, unconscious or perhaps dead, having choked on nothing other than his own tongue as far as I could tell.

Knowing better than to touch the body and later be accused of contributing to his death, I gave the body wide berth and went to the phone where I dialed 911 to summon the police and an ambulance.

In less than five minutes, two police officers and an ambulance attendant were at my door. I let them in and was quick to explain all that had transpired. A young officer and a medic were quick to approach and examine the motionless body. It was confirmed — the intruder was dead.

I sat with one of the officers and gave a complete account of the night. This took no more than 10 minutes, for there was never any suspicion about myself nor the manner in which I had conducted myself during the episode. It was clear that I had never tussled with nor at any time touched the man. This the police were quick to accept based on the evidence. And they were, as it turned out, quite familiar with the dead man and his long record of break-ins and assaults. There was clearly no remorse in that room for the man on the carpet.

After the body had been taken out and I had politely escorted the officers to the door, I mentally steadied myself and decided I must return to bed lest I be too exhausted for work in the morning.

It was then that the unexpected knock came at my door. There stood one of the young officers, with an expression of both astonishment and bewilderment on his face. The medic had found the reason for the intruder's death — the man had indeed choked to death!

For there, lodged deep within my would-be assailant's throat, was my little guardian ivory angel.

THE MAN WITH THE GIFT OF SIGHT

There is a place where the reality of perceptions outshines the perceptions of realities: where the world of our dreams becomes the dreams of the world and where god-like abilities are relative only to those things of which we are normally not capable. I speak of those things that transform us; that distinguish and elevate us from our fellow men. It is of this I speak: for I have known this transformation, and I have tread this path.

Though not with the greatest of facility — no! — such transformations are not necessarily easy, nor wanted. Mine began during my mid-20s, almost 15 years ago. Yet this transformation is far from ended, far from complete. To this I will attest. For my world has changed, and I have arrived at certain of my own conclusions.

I was 26. She, 22. Jude and I were good friends at work, but that was all, there was nothing more. At least not for me. No close relationship had ever developed. I liked her, but I had no feelings of intimate affection for her. But alas, such is really how it all began.

We shared much time together as close friends are wont to do. I have suggested as much by this affirmation of the friendship we enjoyed. Perhaps that in itself was the seed for my attunement: that beginning catalyst.

It was lunch on a late Saturday afternoon. That was all. We had certainly partaken in such minor shared activities often enough. We had seen a matinee together and dining together simply followed. The movie is of no importance, in point of fact, I do not even remember what it was. That is not the issue. Let me just say that it was the conversation — and I use this word lightly, even hesitantly — that followed afterward to which I draw attention.

The talk rambled. Pleasantly. Aimlessly. "Do you think you'll stay with the firm?" "Any plans to travel, or dreams of relocating?" "Long term goals? Any really big dreams?" You know, that kind of talk.

But talk is so often just a mask for other things, is it not? For really, what is being said? So often, communication is what occurs beyond the spoken word; beyond the single dimension of mere words. Yes, I must deem this as so, and I might call myself expert on such things.

For it transpired in a single little moment; a blip of a second when I sat back, entirely relaxed and at ease with not so much as a struggle on my mind that I caught it: a wisp of thought — her thought! It was as if a veil had been dropped, and a little window left her exposed and naked to me. Imagine. The thoughts were directed, focused clearly, plainly, to me; about me: little snippets of information.

"...but it's us...don't you see...open up...in my heart I know...let go...what is it?..."

I stirred, perplexed, reflecting, adjusting, trying to comprehend. It was beyond mere intuition. The thoughts were pure, clear. A portal had somehow appeared into what is typically sacred to any of us.

Surprise and confusion must have shown on me. I

was shocked, even aghast, and it displayed itself, for she asked if something had suddenly entered my mind — it must have appeared to her that I had just seen a ghost. I lied and declared I had been daydreaming. Little could she know. And once more:

"...let me in...where are you?..."

Again. Her thoughts. Had it occurred to me that I were truly in love with her, I might have considered it to be the form of psychic insight lovers develop over several years. But I was not in love with Jude. And this was not an inkling that one gets about certain matters. No — this was the forefront of someone else's mind. That which might be but a moment away from speech or action.

My mind raced. Was it her? Was she causing it? I may have considered it to be something about her but for the fact her demeanor and expressions never altered in consistency of action. Thankfully, that day, we both went our separate ways. For I sought to be alone.

An irony. For in so much of my life I was alone. Always an introvert. Always a thinker. And now I had much to think about. Over a brief period of time the ability shone, developed, grew. Yet, without my yearning for it to do so. I had not the slightest interest in peering into the minds of others. None. But this? An omen. A curse. A mystery.

A fixation! and one of deepening evolvement — for it did grow, and displayed itself well enough during one afternoon at work. Really, the type of work I did is of little importance here. Suffice it to say that it catered to high-end computer usages in the business sector. Jude was the area administrator, and it is pertinent to say that she was stellar at her responsibilities. We each reported to a man by the name of Bob Horvath, someone who I thought had only the finest moral fibre. Well, people can surprise you.

He wanted to speak to me — in private. Nothing more. Soon, we were seated in his office behind closed doors.

He began. "Jude and I have just finished speaking," he said. "We both agreed it would be in each party's mutual interest that she leave the company. She'll be out as of next week."

A surprise to me. I knew Jude and her work well. She confided in me frequently and there was no reason for her to go along with such a decision. Nothing that would lead me to believe she wanted to leave. I explained this.

"Well," Horvath continued, "there are a few details you don't know: things that don't bode well for the company."

It was then that I experienced that glimmering state, that phase of insight. For though he was tight-lipped, his mind was not so closed.

"...little tart...refused me...last chance...didn't come around..."

Dumbfounded, I sat. Admittedly, I was slow to make the connection. He continued the charade through a barely detectable sneer.

"Like I said, I'd like to keep her but..." and his voice trailed off. It now occurred to me, as it does to so many of us under a variety of different situations, just how wrong I could be about others. But one cannot confront someone on the basis of their thoughts. That would be suspicion, unfounded — and ridiculous. Before leaving the room, I caught a final glimpse of the truth to his motives.

"...she'll be gone...get some sweet little thing...willing...wanting..."

So that was it. I left the room feeling sickened by the presence of someone I had once regarded with respect. I had been abruptly disillusioned. Nonetheless, I wanted to speak to Jude. Not that there'd be much of anything I could do for her other than offer my support as a friend.

It was difficult. I knew she didn't have another job to go to, yet she maintained her poise and dignity with perfect aplomb. She accepted my invitation to lunch and we left immediately. She purposely steered the conversation away from the issue of work and her future. Again, I experienced insights that she suspected I knew what had happened. But I played the part of the gentleman and never let on.

And that was it. I will count myself as something of a cad for the fact that I did little to assist her then. I should have taken some action, but instead I sat on the fence not quite knowing what to do. As a result, I was guilty of inaction in the face of this friend's trials and needs.

We returned to work that afternoon but I was increasingly distant; for I was becoming more and more self-consumed. Unable to focus on my job that day, I left early. I was desperate for time alone. I needed to think, just think.

I walked a long distance, passing scores of people from vast assortments of backgrounds and stations in life. The world was so busy. So frantic. A plethora of thought.

"... tax for next year..." "... a hundred bucks to check under the hood..." "...and what the hell did he mean by that..." "... if I don't make the grade..." "...what'll we do now..."

And on and on. Such a busy world, such a kaleidoscope of thought. Foot traffic became mind traffic. I walked through this maze; teeming with the chaos of energy and the ramblings of many, until I could take no more. I cut down a quiet side street to find time and peace alone.

What was this? What was happening? A genetic predisposition? A result of my sensitivity and introversion? It was all so fascinating, and scary. It was incredibly intriguing, yet exhausting. One thing was for certain, this was not my will; not my choice. Still, it was as if I had stepped onto some curious conveyor which was gradually carrying me along; catapulting me forward. But I had no control over it.

That afternoon, I returned to work and locked myself in my office. I was feeling scattered, and reclusive. Anyone watching me would have recognized a change in me. I must have seemed distant, preoccupied. My thoughts were all over the place.

The day came and went when Jude departed. We tried to stay in touch but it was hard on me. I couldn't get into it. Shortly after she left, I gave my notice and left the company as well. I was experiencing such disillusionment from the politics of work knowing people's truer motives and feelings. I just wasn't handling it well. I needed time alone. Even in my personal life, I was isolating myself. The few friends I had were all falling by the wayside. Stress was affecting me. Simple chores such as shopping were becoming tasks.

I needed to get away, to escape. True to my nature, I had to close out the world and withdraw. Fortunately, I could afford the time away. Over the years I had saved and invested a small portion of earnings, so I wasn't too concerned about the lapse in employment. I could take a few months off before becoming concerned about finding work again.

So I took a few weeks and drove — just drove. I headed west toward the Rockies; a place that offered me the finest feelings of solitude in the world. I just needed time. Everywhere I went people's thoughts were there for me. It's amazing the number of trivial little things that ramble around people's minds. It didn't matter whether I stopped for gas, coffee, or just to view off-road tourist attractions. Where ever others were, it was like tuning into some erratic, fleeting, collage of cackling voices. So many of those thoughts were disjointed, undisciplined, inane and downright silly. Every now and then you'd come across someone with focused, controlled and even profound thoughts. But for the most part, most people's minds are very undisciplined. One must wonder about the chaos behind so many free-willed minds.

But it could be humorous. One of my more laughable incidents happened in a restaurant as I sat in a booth right across from a couple in their 30s. They were clearly approaching their anniversary.

"... I'll get her perfume...always loves the perfumes...but God, no more ties...doesn't she know I don't wear ties..." "...he's so difficult to buy for...except for ties...know he loves them...get him one for every day of the week...with luck he won't get me perfume...could fill a swimming pool with the perfumes I don't use..."

Well, it was mischievous but I couldn't help myself. As I stood and prepared to leave the restaurant, I approached them and offered a bit of advice before quickly ducking out:

"Sir, please don't buy her any more perfume, otherwise you may one day find yourself drowning in a swimming pool full of it. And ma'am — he doesn't wear ties!"

They would likely never know just how funny that really was.

My trip to the Rockies helped me that way. It gave me a chance to reflect and indulge in whatever was changing in me. Driving has a way of stretching out the mind just as you are stretching out the highway. And as with that incident in the restaurant, I sometimes found myself relaxing and playing with my newfound skill. There were numerous occasions where I found myself able to contribute little bits of advice to strangers and other travellers.

And so it went. I now had this incredible advantage in gauging people. It could be a tremendous asset. I simply hadn't stopped to consider all the possibilities it could leave open to me — really good possibilities. In business? I would know everything possible to secure sales contracts, make deals and excel at all sorts of business negotiations. As for my personal life, what man wouldn't like to know exactly what some beautiful woman was thinking while he's passing her on the street, all the while making eye contact?

That chunk of time away, reflecting, helped me understand the new world I was living in. Everything had changed. Everything! Yet, it remained a mystery as to how it evolved. But the point was — I could adjust, it was entirely up to me.

The years began to tick by. I went back to work from time to time, finding an assortment of jobs. This was easy for me, since I knew just when and where to look for employment, and just how to conduct myself during interviews. The world was mine, for I had grown well into my gift. But the gift had also grown within me. For as time progressed, no longer did I find myself just reading the surface — oh no! — I had developed to the point where I could see much more within others: their pasts, their psychological make-ups, perhaps even fragments of their very souls.

Yet, it was far from the hit-and-miss stigma attached to fortune telling which I always associated with charlatans. These abilities of mine were pure. Yes — pure, accurate, and absolute. And I — the master.

By the time I was 33, I had relocated to a large eastern city. This in itself must seem somewhat odd considering the many throngs of people and bombardments that awaited me. But I had learned how to manage myself. I knew how and when to pull back to find the quiet times for nurturing my own sanity.

I actually came to enjoy walking through the busy parks, down streets of foot traffic, and through the large shopping malls where hundreds spent their time just wandering. It was most curious what I would find: surface thoughts mocking true-life situations.

For instance, one man I passed walking with his two young children gave me insight into his dire wishes to surprise his young son with a bicycle and a special dress for his daughter. It was touching. He had no reason for the intent of his generosity other than for the love of his kids. But below that, I could see a man who'd had many struggles throughout his own life, including life in foster homes at an early age and some run-ins with the law throughout his teens. Had it not been for meeting a shy and beautiful woman who later became his wife, he likely would have gone into a life of crime. And now, despite facing difficulty with his current job, he put a world of love into his family. It was humbling and touching to see.

Yet, an impeccably dressed young woman who

walked right in front of me revealed someone who had just gotten away with switching price tags to buy a new jacket. The stunt saved her $125, and she had come away feeling quite pleased with herself. But she knew better. She had been raised by loving parents who had always given to her generously along with the highest moral values. She wasn't hurting for money either — and she would disappoint again. What a let down.

Then there was a group of teens mulling around, looking innocent enough. But the knowledge hit me that there would be a fight tonight; a clash between two groups with no excuse to fight other than needing to vent young frustrations and energies. I notified security, but how does one warn about something that hasn't happened yet? Obviously, you can't.

Scads of information came at me: married couples walking hand-in-hand while secretly eyeing and imagining new lovers; business people patting themselves on the back for their ingenuity while destroying the careers of others; teenagers rebelling; others seeking acceptance; identity crisis after identity crisis — "who am I?" "what am I doing here?" On and on it went. Love. Anger. Fear. Emotional setbacks. Scars that would never heal. Wounds that didn't want to heal. People trying to find themselves. Others trying to lose themselves. It was chaos, yet it was almost hypnotic in an operatic sort of way.

And yet, here was I: alone in my life and isolated in my ability, but with a view that perhaps no one had ever before known. I would experience the flood of thoughts and then retreat. Step out, then step back. See and shut out. And continually, I seemed to expand on my own aspects to which I bore witness: to ponder, to reflect. More and more I came to question my place amidst the seekers and the tragically lost. Did the chaos have design? Was the rambling menace of thought and will guided to a point of resolution?

So I too became a seeker — searching through topics of psychology and sociology, theology and philosophy, astrology and the occult. My observations became questions. Soon I was immersed in my own quandary. Was there a greater consciousness? Was it living? Focused with purpose? Perhaps it had always been true for me, but now at least I knew that I was in my own sea of searching — just like everyone else.

The searching continued for years. And though it seems odd that I might have done it, for a while I even went to a counselor to talk out my own fears and thoughts about creation and my place in the cosmos. I never told him about my ability though; to him I was just another patient with a world of questions. I liked him. He had a good heart who felt both empathy and sympathy towards the people who came to him. And I of course, knew all there was to know about him, including his life-long search for place and meaning in his own life. And like everyone else, his mind was sometimes prone to daydreaming. I had some fun with that. We would sit across from one another as I rambled away, and he would stare at me as if he were completely intent on my every word. His mind, however, would drift to topics such as taking his kids downtown, or what he'd be having for supper. So I would abruptly shift gears and ask him if he ever took his kids downtown or what he might be having for supper.

And then, another change.

It presented itself during one long weekend in July. I was 37 now, and had taken a few days to go north and see the beauty of nature in its height of splendour. I was mulling around a small dock by a beautiful lake, making small conversation with other travellers, when I became aware of a profound new feeling. This was unlike the knowing I had experienced during the past years: this did not seem as absolute as a mere tuning into the thoughts of others.

As a young couple climbed into a canoe to go sightseeing around the lake, I became profoundly tuned into the young man, and what was to be his immediate future — and a possible alternate future!

He too had taken time off with his girlfriend to unwind from the strains of school, and an engineering program that, although he despised it, pleased his father's ambitions. This weekend he would cut loose — dangerously. The car they had driven in was his father's, and the youth had loaded the trunk with beer. Tonight he would drink, excessively. And here it was: he would either fall asleep drunk in their motel room, or he would take the car for a joyride to further vent his frustrations. That car ride would end in his death and the crippling of an elderly driver in a head-on collision. As I dwelled on this, I could see the many other lives which would be affected by this tragedy: his father's grief, becoming so severe that he would be unable to return to his own job; his mother's despair, and the blame she would hold for her husband — leading to the collapse of their marriage; the anger of the family of the older man left in a wheelchair from the accident, and his battles with depression; the girlfriend of the youth now failing her own studies and becoming almost agoraphobic. On and on the visions developed. The more I let my mind go, the more I saw the many tragic ramifications of an accident which hadn't even happened.

I never questioned the authenticity of the visions. I knew they were real. I found the car which I knew to be the youth's and waited until no one was around. Then, I punctured all four of the car's tires.

Suddenly, I found myself overwhelmed with a greater peace. Now, the young man and his girlfriend would be seething mad when they discovered the flattened tires, but there would be no accident. By the time a tow-truck arrived to help them in these parts, he would have forgotten entirely about the beer in the trunk. It would throw a kink into their weekend, but the danger was passed, and I felt myself immersed in a feeling of warmth that I had never before known.

It was the most amazing sensation. I now felt as though my own reason for having to escape on this long weekend had been answered — and resolved. I had saved a life and prevented tragedies in the aftermath.

I drove back to the city with a feeling of great elation.

So, I was still evolving. It had been 11 years since my talent had first presented itself, and it gradually continued to develop. I was profoundly different from a decade earlier. And there was no escaping my incredible feelings of warmth and satisfaction. I now felt a peace that I had never experienced. Something other than just my ability was evolving — something deeper within, something of the greater self.

This new dimension to my psyche continued to develop, and so it was that during a short jaunt downtown on a Saturday afternoon some weeks later, I was overcome by tremendous feelings of remorse and regret coming from a raggedly dressed transient sitting across from me on the subway platform. He was in his 40s but he looked over 60. Everything about his life had gone desperately wrong over the past ten years: job loss, crisis in his health, the break-up of his family, and depression. He was beyond destitute, and he knew it. As he quietly sat there, he was considering — quite seriously — making the leap into an oncoming train and ending his pain forever.

But he couldn't possibly have known what I could see. Somewhere out there a daughter who loved him dearly and who he hadn't seen for 15 years searched longingly for him. He might jump today, but if not his destitution would never end unless she found him and helped them complete both of their destinies.

It was easy to know what to do. I approached him and told him how much Charlotte needed him, and that I was here to help him find her. It didn't matter if he wondered how I knew her name, or why a stranger came out of nowhere to offer him help. I bought him a hot meal, helped him into a men's hostel where they assured me they would assist him, and then, out of my own pocket I called every newspaper in the area to place ads on his behalf reaching out to his daughter. On one of those calls to a large daily paper I had that magical feeling all over again: the connection would be made. She would see the ad and find him. His life, and hers, would return to one of salvation and grace.

And again I had that feeling of complete well being in my own heart.

No longer would I be a mere observer. I would find a role as an active participant in people's lives, gently persuading them to make the right choices, even in the simplest of ways. I would be there to encourage the good choices, even if it meant manipulating circumstances to serve a better end. Would I be playing God? In all my searching, the teachings of so many indicated that nothing came by accident, and that we are all here to use our gifts.

In retrospect one might wonder, would I not use all that I was capable for my own good?; my own selfish gain? To this I can only say that where one does not have a heart of greed or will of malice, temptations are not a thing of question. For "as a man thinketh in his heart, so is he." And in this I have learned much of myself, and have come away proud.

But to serve myself? No — not I. I would assist people where ever I would go, where ever I could, whenever it was necessary. I could help prevent tragedies, or heartbreak. I could help guide people away from the wrong choices; the hurtful choices — those things down their paths that they would never see, but that I would know as certainties.

Perhaps then, there was a greater will. Perhaps I was on the road to the Oneness that ultimately waits to embrace us all. I would play my small part as we all have the option of doing, each in our own way.

And I would find my place.

A GOTHIC TALE OF MADNESS

Madness! I feign it not. Sanity? It has been mine to have, to cherish, to hold tenaciously. Has it not? Well, if that were not so, why then have they sought to steal it from me? Steal it! Yes! Them! They! They who would rob it — and more — from me. That and the spring from which it was born. And if one hasn't their sanity, their mind, then what have they, I ask? Nothing! A soul? I think not. For what can be the essence of the soul with no earthly mind to manage and nurture it? Aah, so they would be robbers of my soul. Yes, I see it as so. Thieves and criminals of such insidiousness that God alone might comprehend. And judge! Oh yes. Yet these are bigger questions, I agree. But really they are all one question, just one. I know it. I know.

My body? Ruined. The castle of my mind, the warehouse of my soul. All gone. Perished. Destroyed by those barons of dark and unequivocal evil. Wrecked! Broken! Torn apart by the dark lords. That is all, yet it is not. And the question? Aah-hah! Yes, the question! Blast it! Blast it to God. For it is not a question at all. No, instead it is simply their plaything. The means by which they allow themselves to begin their game, their ploy to have you do that which you promise yourself you will not do: anticipate and loathe, wait and shudder, tremble and quake. I know. Oh God how I know. For I did anticipate. And I did loathe. And my shudders were the brevity between my placid yesterdays and the timelessness of my unholy screams. Yet here I am! And I am not mad. I am not!

Do not let yourself be fooled either. For they will move you, persuade you, have you be their pawn. Yes, They will coerce! — oh, those clever ones. They will have you think that you see clearly; that their way is the right way, the only way. And really, who is to say? Not I. No, never. I shall not put myself on the pedestal to judge nor condone as they do. For I am nothing. Nothing! But they? Oh, they are so different. So apart. They need not understand the mind of a man. And yet they are so expert at breaking that very thing.

How long ago it was. Or was it? Ah, you see, the mind does falter. It does skip a beat. Was it a thousand moons? A thousand years? Or a simple fraction of a single dawn? I know not. Nor shall I say that I care. And yet truly, my woes have just begun. For time did stand unmoving. Isolated. And I was its lone captive. But I do remember... things... some things.

The river. That much I remember. Moving. Gentle. Blue. So calm, so tranquil. Another reality even yet. And the sky! There too! Another expanse of blue — wide, open, with little works of cloud. All so gentle. All so serene. Not far from the river was the house. Not large, but home to the few who might help me, love me, watch over me. Our clothes we washed by the riverside. A gentle memory indeed. On bright and warmer days, such as it was, we would cook outside and smell the scent of gentle blossoms mix with the wood smoke that would tempt our hunger. And there was laughter! Now, after all this, it is hard to believe that there was laughter. And talk of pleasant things: all bits of pause in a world waiting to spin out of control.

And a fox! Yes. I do remember it. We all saw it but it was I who noticed it first. Not long did we see it, but it was there, across the riverbank. It stepped out from the bushes and stood, watching us. Just watching. Then, it was gone! All in a blur. Oh how I miss that little fox. I wonder what he thought that day. Did he know something? Was he an omen? I cannot possibly know. But there he was. And now? Did he run off to find his mate? To nurture his young? Did he marvel at the beauty of the river and the simplicity of the sky? Did he too smell the blossoms and feel the temptation of our food? Where is he now, that little fox? Oh, little fox. I would wish you well, but what is it that you may have wished me?

Doesn't matter. For after all, he is the fox, a creature of the forest. And I? Just a man — less so! Aah, did I speak of the forest just now? You see how memories are so attached, intertwined? Yes, that is the way of the forest and its glade, the river and its bank, the Earth and its children. All attached. All one. And yet all so separate and apart. But now you may think me rambling. And what of it? I should be allowed as much. There was a time as a child when they thought me mute. Can you believe? Yes, me! But I was not of course, just quiet. Just so very, very quiet. Not insecure or troubled mind you. Just serene, and thoughtful, and quiet. But this is different now. Now I allow myself words, many words. The mind can be focused so. It is true. Look at me. I speak and I am.

But did I not have you wondering about that river and its little friend the fox? Well, there is more. Much much more. But why should I bore you about the little things: the roots we fed on, the fish we pulled from the river, oh! and the chestnuts — and how well they roasted. But I promised not to bore. Well, I promise I will not. I surely will not.

Let us talk of the house. It was not large, but it was so very well constructed. Oh how true. It held us all: six of us. But that really is the joke isn't it? I mean, that it did hold six — and how many more — is the very point of the matter. The sheer inventiveness of it! To think of the brilliance of those masters of stone masonry and carpentry that built it. Sheer genius! You see, it held six and still would have held more! For that was its great secret. Beyond certain walls, beneath certain floorboards, and supported above certain ceilings where you would have thought no room existed, a man could be hidden for a week! Yes, two men even. With hiding room for water and food to sustain them in such a desperate situation. And if you were nimble, you could even move from one hiding place to another from behind a wall or above a ceiling. Yes, that was how cleverly they had constructed the place. Why, even the rats would have had trouble locating those special places. Aah, but we are not speaking of rats, are we? No, we are referring to something far more cunning, and loathsome and devious — men! Yes, that is the way of things.

And that is where they found me. As if they knew. Cunning fiends. But it was just a matter of time, wasn't it? Well, so now does it seem. In my heart of hearts I knew they would find me. But it is far too easy to look back and speak of that which has now taken place. To look forward and know... well, that is another matter.

It was late in the day, but the sun was still warm. The leaves were only beginning to turn their warm golden hues of late summer. So beautiful. So serene. But my love for the wonders of the Earth are not the issue. No. There have been far more serious matters at hand for me, so let me recall, and recite! Well, somehow we knew that they would come. And come they did. It was only a matter of time, but listen to how I repeat myself. I must think... focus. We stayed close to the house knowing they would come. For it was our arc; our ship to save us. But again, I am side-tracked! The day — that day! We had bathed in the river, we had eaten, we had taken rest. If there can be moments of reprieve on this Earth that come close to paradise then that day was it. But it is not uncommon for some to remember times of great bliss and beauty just before their world has been shorn to tatters.

The horses. We heard them from a distance as we knew we might. That was only a minor blessing, having some notice beforehand. There were five or six mounts, but I must say it sounded like the King's entire army hastening in our direction. The others all bid me to quicken. And yet I must confess, for a moment I was frozen and could not move. Such is the way fear can affect one. But then! — my senses took hold and I was afoot. To the house! To the house! Not a moment to spare. My hiding place in waiting, and now I was to become its captive as fate's wheel spun 'round and 'round deciding my outcome.

From within I could barely hear their voices. They had indeed come for me. But the others, my friends, would not betray me. There was talking, not demanding but authoritative. I could not fathom the reply. Then there were other voices joining in, friendly, persuasive. Aah! My companions. Convincing. Manipulating. Thwarting the soldiers and hunters of men. Then, more commotion — and alas! Entry into the house! Aah. So the scent was indeed strong in their nostrils. Well, let bile rise up in their throats. I would not be found! I would not!

Marching through the house now... room to room. Banging on the walls, the floors, the ceiling... and listening! Ah, those clever ones. They seek to hear echoes or hollow points behind the boards. Well, damn them to hell. They will hear nothing. Nothing! Lest for my heart which may betray me with its thunderous beating. But I will not move. I will not betray myself. Be still my quaking body, please be still.

Room to room, again and again. Devils! They will not give up so easily I see. More banging on the walls. Listening. Feeling. Ears pressed against wood. Then, some move outside while others remain inside.

Aah, all in working unison now. So determined. So bent on finding space where there should be no space. Well, I will be still. My trembling body and quivering lips will not be heard. Nor my heart, which does its best to burst from my chest. Still. Be still. Very very still.

An order! I heard it. The group commander has barked an order. I am not here! This is not the place! An error? Faulty information. Wrong assumptions. I do not exist! Blessed God. They are taking leave. More commotion. Someone is angry, time has been wasted. Heavy footsteps vacate the house. Oh Lord, these tortuous moments will soon be rewarded with my freedom. Sweet victory. It will soon by mine in this little war of nerves. Liberty awaits!

Now I hear the horses. Leaving, they are leaving. Galloping, riding off — I can barely hear their sounds now, fading. A few more moments. And then? Silence, just wonderful blessed silence. But wait! Better to wait a few moments more, to be sure. Let them be long gone. Please, please, please. I have waited this much. Another matter of seconds will be nothing.

So? Well, nothing now. Just the sound of my companions resuming their talk. Soon they will call for me and knock the secret knock to notify me that all is well. Aah-hah! There it is. They call! and the knock... it is true. I am free to leave. The dark moments are passed.

I stand slowly now within my tiny space. My joints are a little sore. That's okay, hardly a price to pay for my freedom. I open the secret wall, and with my back to the room, I ease out to greet the others and... Aah! What is this! What leering treacherous face is this that stares back at me? A guard! And another! They are upon me! Oh Mother of God how could this be? I am betrayed. Deceived! The King's guards are upon me.

I am captured!

Such was the day of my arrest. Arrest, yes, but do not ask for what, because in times such as these it matters not. It matters only if they find you guilty, and if not, well, that may not make a difference either. Then they may wish for you to confess anyway. And that is a far far worse thing than being guilty. If you are guilty you may face a quick death — or you may not. Hah! That is the question. But to face confession, well then, God be with you. For to face confession, you will be tested beyond anything you would have thought possible. And you will learn of your limits. Do you doubt? Look at me! Just look! I am testament for what I speak.

And of my betrayers? They hardly matter now, do they? After all, I cannot condemn them all. Surely that is a fair thing to say. I would not believe that all were involved to see me taken. That I will accept. We shared too too much and became far too close for such a thing to occur. But perhaps one or two of them? Well, here I am, there must be some truth to it. Although, how can I know their conditions of my arrest. Perhaps they were threatened. Perhaps they were just very very frightened. Yes, that I would understand. Fear can make one do many things. Many odd things. Things that you would not feel are within you, but alas! there you go. And you see, it is all a matter of knowing how to manipulate a man's fear. For then, you have him, haven't you? All of him. Heart and soul.

The first night of my arrest was so cold, so lonely, so full of uncertainty and fear. I was read the charges, but they matter not. Not, I say, for I am no criminal. I am not. But why should you believe me? Well, all so often our fates are decided not so much upon our actions but upon our inactions; not so much upon truths but on perceived truths. Yes! And I would know, for that night, after listening to the charges filed against me, I was cast into a rotting filthy prison with nothing more than watery soup to satiate my thirst and hunger. My sleep — restless, disturbed. And what else would it be? I had once lived the life of a man, in freedom and with as much liberty as I could have. Then? Running, hiding, terror, imprisonment, and a life that came to a halt. So then my dreams became disturbed. All so very very disturbed. But life is a dream, isn't it? Oh, if that were only true, for I would pray that I could wake from it. Oh yes, I would awaken — now.

Well, that night came and went. Sleepless. Hungry. But who should care? The next morning my jailers came calling. They led me away, in leg irons, out of my cell. Was this to be freedom? Hardly. Such is not the way of humankind. There was justice to be served. I have been guilty of nothing and yet I am aware that justice sought me out. I was taken in front of the magistrate, in what I can only call a fool's court. Here, I was led before the robed powers that would cast the pebble of my fate. And in their fool's ritual of righteousness I was made a mockery. A mockery! The charges were read again. Again! But again I say that I have been guilty of nothing. Would I confess? Yes! This is what they wanted. What they expected. Confess! Can you believe? I would have none of it. "Innocent!" exclaimed I. Well, I was given council, but it was all a farce. My council was cut from the same cloth as my accusers. Yet, truly, I have always been innocent.

Does not matter. Not now and not then. Again the charges were read. Again I was given the chance to plead my guilt. But I would not. Was I stubborn? Was I the fool? I should have trembled at the scene, but I was aghast at the absurdity of it and I stood my ground. Was I aware of the consequences they asked me? Was I aware of the seriousness of the offence to which I denied? Blast this mockery I charged! But what was the use? I was only one against their many. A single speck of dust of a man resisting an onslaught of inevitable madness.

So then, so gently, so woefully did my council encourage me to reconsider. I was given a moment to think this out. Hah! What was more serious I challenged, suffering the persecution of guilt or that of innocence? And do you see now as I saw then, that no matter what I might have said I was to be the plaything of their game? Well, I was right, was I not? Again the damned question! Again my declaration of complete innocence! Again and again. Well, this is how they put you to the question...

For it was then that I was taken, taken to see... Yes! Yes, you know... to The Tower, and there to see the instruments...

...of my torture.

The Tower. Can you think of a more horrid thought? A more horrid place? Dark. Cold. Damp. Infested with rats and vermin. Oh yes, I had heard the rumours of the rats: there to dine on what remained of bodies yet alive. And I had heard of the many horrible devices used to break the bodies of criminals and heretics. As a younger man I had shuddered at the tales I had heard of The Tower: of people torn apart on the rack, of those boiled alive, of others slowly pressed to their deaths under hundreds upon hundreds of pounds of weight until their rib cages broke through. Mutilations, shattered limbs, scalded flesh. I had heard all these things. And this was where I was destined.

Well it is the very bowels of hell itself. And one can feel that there are ghosts here, all vile and cold. One can feel them. They are real. The air is heavy and putrid with the stench of death. For as I entered, I was overwhelmed with nausea and my stomach heaved. Such is the tangible reek of it. The stones? They cry out with the blood and screams of many.

For the walls are built very thick, so as to conceal the torment and screams of its prisoners, and yet I heard screams. Screams upon screams, and the beggings of desolation and mercy. But in this place there is no mercy. Here, there is no hope. None. God himself has ceased to exist here. There is only pain upon pain and despair within despair. And I saw things. Many horrible things.

They were laid out for me, these things. A tour. My would-be tormentor? He stood hooded, unsympathetic, unflinching in this, his domain, as both keeper and macabre host to all these vile instruments that all the darkness in man could dare conceive: Skull Crushers, the Gridiron, Scavenger's Daughter, various assortments of knives and pincers which glowed red in well-tended hot coals, and the Boots! the dreaded Boots! Oh! these dastardly villains. Monsters! We ventured further and now, yes! I heard screams. Unfathomable, inhuman. Oh, the madness. But what was I to do? What would they have me say?

It was afterward that I again was brought to my little cell and again given the watery soup. I would be left there overnight, doubtless to give thoughts to the things I had seen and the sounds I had heard. Well, I ate the soup and lay back, trying to rest. But I had nothing, nothing but thought. And that is what they must have wanted of me: to think. Think and contemplate and fathom all the horrible things of my day's visit. Aah! But my mind floundered. It dwelt not on these things, but on sweeter things of my past. And that is curious, is it not? That a man facing such dire consequences should think of things more pleasant. Well, that is what I did. I found myself remembering the flowering blossoms of spring. Blossoms! Yes! Can you believe? It is true. From just months ago, the beautiful scents and colours of the vineyards and gardens. Ooh, so soothing, so tranquil. And honeybees! I did remember them also. If ever there was a creature on God's earth that is blessed, it must be the honeybee. For what a duty it must be to visit the beauty of new blossoms with each awakening new day. And aah! but for the sweetness of smell and taste of honey. And on and on. Oh but to visit those sweet little flowers again. But... aha! I have done it, have I not? I have found my little garden within. Well, it is true. And I would visit it yet again and again, that beautiful garden and her lovely blossoms. I was to find that I would need my little garden.

And so on the following morn I was brought before the magistrates and their mockery of justice. Again I was encouraged to plead my guilt. Only not so gentle this time. Now, there was a greater sense of urgency in their demands. My council? A mere plaything of their whims. To me? Nothing! Less than nothing. Would I confess?!

"But of what, my lord? I confess I am a man who breathes the air and seeks to find beauty in each new day."

Well, they asked had I not seen the vile instruments of The Tower, and was I not afraid that I might taste their sweet caresses? And of course, I had become very very afraid. But I would not yield! I would not! Again my council pleaded with me. Again the charges. Again my denial to be a part of this absurd circus. Someone shouted "defiant fool!" at me. And perhaps they were right. For the sands in my little hourglass had run out.

And I was handed my sentence.

I was to be taken back to The Tower, though not as a mere observer. My penalty? Harsh. Cruel. Impossible to fathom. I stood, listening to the charges as they were read for the final time; listening to my sentence; observing the bland and matter-of-fact tones as my sentence was read. Grey faces with cold bloodless eyes stared back at me. Now the severity of this reality was before me. I trembled. I quaked. I felt a weak little voice rise in the back of my throat; whimpering, like that of a child; a squeak of a sound. At this moment I knew not myself. And I have never felt so utterly alone as in that moment of time. Now I truly felt I knew the obstacle of my own humanity, for it stood before me and I could not help but stare back at it: it was fear. Numbing. Nauseating. Thus, I listened to the sentence as it was read before me:

"...and ye are to be escorted back to The Tower in leg irons and chains where ye will be given time to consider your obstinacy before the King's court in the holding place known as 'Little Ease'. By this ye shall know the penalty of your hiding. Here ye shall stay for 10 days and 10 nights and not be given release until the end of

that time. Upon your release from the Ease ye shall be given one hour to consider your insult upon the court and allowed that time to make confession to the charges before ye. If you do not submit to the court's truth then ye shall experience the Boots for a period as set forth by your jailer. By this ye shall know the penalty of your running. Upon this time ye shall again be given time to reconsider your affront to the King and his rule. Then, ye will be given time to taste the caress of the Duke of Exeter's Daughter. Afterward you will be escorted to die, broken upon the wheel. By this ye will have served your sentence. After your death your remains will be cast upon fire so that ye may be returned to the dust of your making. So decideth the court. May God have mercy on your soul."

Now, I slunk to my knees but the guards came and lifted me to my feet. And thus I faced the end of humanity in both myself as well as in the eyes of those around me. This could not be. This was a dream. It must be. And I must awake. Wake! Now, please please wakc. But I did not. Then, if I could not wake up, let my soul fly free from my body. Let them twist and burn and tear every limb of me, but let my soul be free. Aah, but that too would not come to pass. I stared into a void of emptiness and saw only fear, intense tangible fear, staring back. I was alone.

The guards wasted no time with me. Immediately I was bound in irons and chains. I was asked a question: Did I have anything to say to the court? Well, what was I to do, declare my innocence? I am innocent but

I am now bound in chains. I could not mutter a word. In that single moment I became a stooped-over, half shell of a man who could not so much as think to speak. I was to be whisked off to the dungeons of The Tower and my accusers and sentencers would go to their homes for hot broth and supper. The blemishes upon their souls for this travesty of justice would be nothing compared to the screams of my anguish and pain. God damn them. God damn them all.

So, I was taken to The Tower. And how do you think I was treated? Do you think that they serve well those prisoners who are bound for death? Well, they do not. I was spat upon and made a spectacle as I was hauled through the streets like a wild animal. Flaunted. Teased. Ridiculed. But that is a small matter, for I was escorted straightaway to the first of my destinations — Little Ease.

And what is Little Ease? Well, have you ever tasted darkness? I mean real, tangible black darkness that can wrap itself around you like a cloak? Little Ease is nothing more than a cell, but a very very special cell. Imagine... it is built into the stone masonry deep within The Tower. And it is oh so specially built, for it is little more than one pace in each direction. Yes! That is all! Less than four feet square and perhaps eight or nine feet high. Why, a man hasn't room to lie down nor even sit on the cold stones properly. And when they close you in you are completely enveloped in darkness. Total, absolute darkness. There is no light at all. None. And the air is stale for it only seeps its way in through small vents built into the stone. Yet it is in this hellish hole that I stayed for 10 days and nights with nothing more than my own thoughts to keep me company: thoughts of those things which I yet faced. Cramped. Cold. Dizzy. Unable to rest. Unable to move. Was it hour one? Or day one?...

My legs, numb. No space to move. I stood, feeling the darkness, feeling the walls of my cell, reaching up to the ceiling. Getting oriented in my little prison. But I could not stand for long. My feet ached. My spirit, diminished. So I crouched, crunched up on the cold stone. So alone. Nothing to do but endure, and think, and listen — aah! Silence. Complete here, in this place. I might sleep, if it were not for my dreams. Things that I fear. But that will come later. For now? Thoughts. Feelings. Exploring within. And the pain of time...

Aha! I have been drifting. Not asleep, I do not think, but somewhere. How long, how long? Already my eyes crave light. Any light, small though it may be. Wait! A face! Yes, that is where my thoughts were, though sleep or not. And such a gentle face. Kind, loving, my soothing vision — Anne. We had barely known one another. An interlude, so brief. Yet here was love. Unconditional, eternal. How is it that I have placed her out of my mind until now? My trials. They have contorted the essence of me. But now I have her back, if nowhere else then at least in my mind. That is something. Truly it is. So, to sweeter thoughts, sweeter memories...

Town. A beautiful spring day. Warm. Sweet. The

promise of warmer weather to come. A gentle stroll through the streets. Faces, many of them. There is some singing a little way in the distance. I listen but I go the opposite direction — toward the market. The smell of fresh bread carries me. Here there are more people, bakers and farmers and craftsmen selling their trades and goods. Something moves me forward, toward a table of pottery and candles and cloth. And there she is! Someone like no other. Beautiful. Serene. Our eyes meet and... lock. Oh, she is so young. But a flower! And a gentle smile appears on her face, and then on mine. My heart moves. She is a wonder. Truly she is.

Hunger! It has snapped me out of my reverie. I was drifting, in such a sweet little memory. But I am not skilled at meditation. I do not stay in that blessed state for long. Reality bears too heavily upon me. It would have me sit up and feel all things that are real. But what is real? My thoughts? My dreams? Or my torments? Well, they must feed me, mustn't they? No. That is another dream. Others have been left in the prisons to die and rot. Why should I be fed if this is my fate. And I have not been here long, well, I do not think but I do not know.

My reality is this, now. My joints are numb. I must stand, I must! Painful. But I must make myself move. Oh God! I need to stretch out. But there is that damned stone wall within my darkness. And I must endure. I do rise, so slowly. I question if my body will last. Or my mind. But what choice have I? Well, where my mind survives my body must follow.

And the darkness. It is like a blanket. So dark, so dark...

But this time I have been asleep. Sweet sweet sleep. But for how long? Who is to know? It feels like many hours, or days. Such a blessing is sleep. My body is crumpled on the floor, and stiff. I must have slept at length. And... what is this! What is this! By my feet? Bread! Blessed bread. So I am to be fed after all. And I am ravenous with hunger. Ravenous. So ravenous.

So, is this to be the way of my suffering? To relish that I might sleep and hope it lasts indefinitely? And to be grateful to the heavens for a loaf of stale bread? What am I to do but endure? I must endure. I must, I must. But then, why? Why must I endure? To suffer greater pains. And to die, as we all must. Yes! That is true, is it not? We will all die. But my death will not be as my maker had intended for me, not natural, not at peace nor at ease. Hah! There is irony in that is there not? And as for what my maker wants of me, well, how am I to know? How really. Oh for God. Oh but to know his kindness and his will. I myself do not believe in a cruel god. I cannot! I do not. My God is one of mercy and peace. Yes. It is men who are cruel. Cruel and deceptive and unjust. And no god who could create the spring blossoms and the scent of wild berries in the field or the face of an angel could be cruel. But then, if I say that I loved this woman, for an eternity, for all time, even though we scarcely spent any time alone together... Aah, but what is the point of this inner torment? If I allow myself such anguish then they have truly robbed me of my soul. And they will not! They will not, I swear, no, never.

And so had my thoughts and my pains and my dreams carried me through Little Ease, that deplorable place. 'Twas not a prison at all, but something that cannot be described. Loneliness upon loneliness. Blackness; total, complete, smothering. Cold. Damp. No way to rest. Impossible to stretch and move. My body became weak and stiff. My mind? The shadows within me felt like screaming, and at times I did scream. And screamed and screamed. But to no avail. There was no mercy. Not for me. Nothing, lest for my sweet thoughts of Anne and better times. By the time they came for my release I was crumpled, starved, weak. My feet and legs, swollen from standing and crouching for so so long, trying ever to gain some comfort. But finding none. Begging to see light and yet frightened by it. Feeling the need to run and thrash about but instead, once freed, I lay on the outer stone floor whimpering. Hungry. Beaten. Stripped of all strength. Where has man found it within himself to invent such a hideous place? I cannot even begin to explain my feelings of despair and loneliness. I was the only man alive in the world. Alone. Little Ease destroys the soul. Strong though you think you may be, that little prison will make you as weak and humble as the day you were born, unable to face the world and frightened by all, by everything. So cruel, so cruel.

And yet there was so much more in store for me.

When I was freed, they were waiting like the harsh and brutal beasts that I knew them to be. I could barely respond to their presence I was so exhausted. And that is what they would have wanted of me. Compliance. That I would be at their disposal; body, heart and soul. But they were wrong! A man is not so easily beaten. Or is he? Perhaps I do not know. How, really, do we know our limits until we have been tested? How really? Well, I was given just a little bit of water and that is all. For they would have wanted me in my weakened state. That way, one is more inclined to do what they want, say what they want. But not the truth. Never the truth. No, for what they seek is that you be what they want you to be. The magistrate and my jailer were there. I knew that this would be only a short reprieve, for once again, I was tasked to answer their questions. Make confessions. True or not, they wanted only to hear what they would choose to hear.

And so it began, the dreadful questioning. And now again I declared my innocence, though this time, in such a weak and trembling voice that I did not recognize it to be my own. Was I not encouraged by Little Ease, they asked. "But of course," it has given me to see the greater cruelty of man while guiding me to find some little island of solace deep within. Was I not afraid of that which I was yet to face? "Terribly afraid, sir!" I replied. "But my fear is born of my innocence and the knowledge that ye care not about such things." "Confess!" they cried. "Do not make yourself out to be this fool. Do you not see what follows? Confess!" Again and again they implored me. Again and again I denied them. "Mockery," I charged. "Fool," they countered. "Do not make us continue, tell all damn you!" "Tell all?" I queried. "I was born, I have lived, and I shall die! I have walked the forest glade and I have smelled the rich soil of farmers' fields. I have felt the sun and tasted the wind. I have known the laughter of children and felt the kindness of strangers. Tell all?" I repeated. "Well, that is all, truly that is all."

Did not matter, as I knew it would not. For my little hour of reprieve and questioning was done. And now? Now, I was to face the second part of my sentence, that which truly did make me shudder, that which brought the taste of fear to the back of my throat: the dreaded Boots.

Here, they promised me, I would learn the meaning of pain. And they did not lie. First, I was securely strapped to a hard wooden bench. Then, each of my legs were inserted into the likes of two hideously thick spongy leather boots which rose beyond the calves of each leg. Each of these contraptions were held in place by iron frames to keep the legs secure. Soon now it would begin: the pouring of scalding hot water over the thick heavy leather and boiling the flesh of my legs within. Now, I was arrested by panic. Now I quaked out of control; trembled like a leaf in the wind — but the strappings on the bench held me fast. Nausea hit me. I could not face this. I would not get through this. But here I was! And again the damned questioning began...

"Do you speak?" they asked.

"Why do you torment me so?" I implored.

"Speak now! Confess all!" they screamed.

"Oh God have mercy on me!" I wailed. "Mercy, mercy!"

"Save yourself this punishment," they persisted, "confess!"

"But there is nothing for me to say," I whimpered.

"Do you have us proceed then?" they continued.

"Oh Lord," I declared. "Save me from this agony, do not forsake me!"

But alas, I was forsaken. For no more words were spoken. All I saw was the magistrate motion to the demon in the hooded black mask. Beads of sweat trickled down my brow. A child's cry rang out from me. A shudder ran through me... and it began.

When the first draught of boiling water was poured over The Boots, hot steam rose with the rancid stench of old leather and its history of previous agonies. My legs felt as if they were on fire! I felt the destruction of a body that once had been young and strong. Screams bellowed from deep within me. I gnashed my teeth and thrashed violently, locked steadfast to my grisly fate. Insane wails echoed from my being. A heavy sweat covered my body, and the questioning continued.

"You can cease this pain now! Tell us!" the magistrate demanded.

"Oh God, Oh God do not forsake me!" I pleaded through my pain.

"Damn your soul! You are guilty are you not? Let us hear!"

"I am the innocence of birth," I whimpered.

"Fool! Damn liar! Your pains have scarcely begun! Confess!"

"I am a child of the Lord!" I declared. "Oh why does He forsake me?"

With this, the magistrate motioned to the gaoler to continue. More boiling water was poured over The Boots, and I heard unfathomable screams which I knew to be my own. I felt the skin and meat of my feat and legs whither and burn. Then, suddenly, mercifully, I was arrested back to a beautiful spring day and the gentle scent of lilacs...

We were walking, hand in hand. Although I thought I knew her beauty, I seemed to see something new and more beautiful about her each time I gazed upon her. A few little freckles danced across her cheeks. Her hair held a radiance as if the sun rose through her. And her skin? As pure and silken as the beads of an early spring dew. Yet, my attraction to her was more than that of a mere man. I had never doubted the power nor the existence of love under God's beautiful skies, for now love had been guided into my simple humble life. Now, I was shown the true power and strength behind this most wonderful thing. And I felt as new to the Earth and its beauty as man's very first day.

We spoke of little things, as new loves are wont to do: the music of crickets, the magic of the wind, the blessedness in a simple moment of being — all these things and so much more. We knew one another completely, as if our time together had been the journey of so many life times before. Here was bliss. For she was the answer to all the questions within me which I never knew I carried.

But my beautiful little reverie was stolen from me. I roused from my dream to find that wine was being forced down my throat to force my recovery back to the conscious world. From my blessed walk with God's angel I was again in the dungeons of The Tower with my tormenters. They were slapping my cheeks and persisting with more wine. Now I was returned to them and my agonies. Again I was their pawn, their victim. And they were robbing something from me greater than they could fathom. But I would not give them the satisfaction of knowing! They would break my body, my mind and my soul, but I would never let them discover just what they had truly taken from me. And in this, I found a little renewed strength — and sadness.

They continued their dreadful doings. Time froze as I discovered how a simple moment could become an eternity. The questioning rang and reverberated through my being. Yet! they heard nothing of what they wanted to hear from me, lest for my cries. Finally, I again lost all sense of consciousness and fell into a blackness where even dreams did not exist.

When I awoke, I was free of The Boots, for I was lying on a wooden plank and free of bondage. They had stopped. It would not do to have the prisoner die before his sentence was fully executed. As for the absence of chains and tethers, how was I to escape? My legs were ruined. I was crippled. Pain continued to sear through my being and I was weak as a lamb. I moaned. I wept. But how does this matter? For this is everything they sought of me: my destruction.

Eventually, a few morsels of food were forced down my throat. Little bits of bread and salted meat, then a little water. I had to be alive to endure my final end. Thus I was left to rest a little longer, gathering strength. They seemed just to leave me, but I knew that I was still very much the focus of their interest. I thought I heard some discussion about me, but what of it? Would they make me talk or not? Would I survive my next ordeal or die before the sentence was completed? Surely, a man in a trade such as the executioner must take great cares to see that the full punishment is exacted as set forth by the court. After all, we mustn't have some poor wretch dying before their agonies and torments were maximized for the sake of justice!

But again I feel my thoughts are rambling. Though, why not? Still, this hardly matters. And despite my pains I find myself questioning that which does matter — if anything. I have given much of my life to the Lord and yet he has forsaken me upon my own little cross. I have been there for him in all my little ways and yet where was he in my time of need? Ah! Do you hear the cynicism in me? Well it is not a characteristic of me, I assure you it is not. But I have endured much. And we must not forget all that I am here for! In truth, my body — racked in agony — will not forget. But really, need I go through all the vile and ugly details? I say not.

I did face the Duke of Exeter's Daughter. She is quite the lady, for her caresses are indeed unlike that of any other woman a man would care to know, for she is The Rack: another abominable creation of man's unlimited dark imagination. For hours on end I tasted her! Twisting and tearing my joints and ligaments. Agonies within agonies. Endless and barbaric. Screams within screams. Fainting away and hoping never to recover, yet always brought about by the skill of my gaoler who knew my limits before death better than I. And the magistrate and his questions! Questions and accusations. On and on. Well, they too finally came to an end, though the pain did not. Though I do not make myself out to be a brave man. Oh no. Quite the contrary. For I said many many things to bring the pain to an end. But perhaps not what they wanted to hear. Or perhaps I did. Who is to know? Though this I do know: if they sought accomplices to my alleged crime, no names did I mention. No! Not one. Not a single one. Yet in my heart, she has been with me in my trials always.

And now? Yes, now. I face the final curse of my dreaded sentence: to be broken upon The Wheel. But not just a process of death. Oh, no! To be put to this grisly end would deny many the entertainment and titillation of their dulled senses. So I am to be the spectacle! The local entertainment.

And this is where I stand now...

There is a sea of faces. Hundreds to be sure, perhaps a thousand. The stage, the scaffold, is in the centre of the lusting hungry mob. It is here that I am being led. The gaoler and his assistant await my presence on the stage. They stand hooded, unwilling to reveal their true identities. Cowards! I say. I am exposed, yet my tormenters hide behind dark cloth. My body is completely broken, and yet I am bound in leg irons and chains. I am their prisoner. There are shouts and taunts and heckles, but this too matters not. For a man such as I who has endured as much cares not about the naivete of simple words. An irony for me though... to have my life ended in the midst of such crass ignorance. Yet, this impudence and insult is as much a part of my sentence as my physical suffering.

As weak and broken as my body is now, I stretch and twist and contort myself in a desperate attempt to see if there is that one person in the mob. My eyes search over the sea of faces, but it is difficult. Such commotion. Such madness. And I haven't the strength to persist. I do not see the one fair and blessed face that I would die for. She is not here.

Soon it will begin, this dreaded end. I will follow many a criminal and heretic in this manner which I die: to be bound upon the flat wheel with my limbs hanging over the outer rim. Then, the executioner will proceed to shatter each and every limb of my body with a heavy iron bar. Only if I endure this agony will I make it to the final blow — that which crushes my breast and stops my heart. Oh Lord, oh Lord if you are still with me then spare me this final end. Spare me! For I am not strong enough nor brave enough to face this. I am not. I am only a man, and now I question even that.

The crowd begins to build into a frenzy. Such blood lust. Such desire to see a man die in this most wretched manner. There are guards stationed around the scaffold to control the mob: to keep people at bay from the place where I am to die.

There is music. Yes! Can you believe? And laughter! And the smell of food! Madness! Oh, the madness! What a world it is that a man as fiercely sane as myself must die at the hands of such maddened monsters. But I must resign myself to this fate. For there will be no blessed angel to save me.

I am bound naked to the wheel. Not the slightest bit of cloth to give me dignity. Nothing. I am exposed as the day of my birth. Now soon, so soon shall it begin, my dying agonies. Again, I raise my head to get a glimpse of just one face, to know that she is here with me. But I see nothing. She is not here. She will not be with me in my final moments.

It begins now. There are words spoken from my stage. Words, just words. They matter not, of course.

For all that I have endured I might consider myself the master of understanding the power of words. And these are empty, hollow. The unruly mob stills. There is quiet now. My time is here. Now they will begin.

My executioner and his assistant command the stage. I am the centre of attention yet they command all. Well, that is the madness that I might expect. My body grows both tense and numb. It is true that death focuses the mind. How did I come to be here? I had lived the good and peaceful life and yet now I am to die horribly. Oh, but to turn back the sands and relive those choices. But it is too late for that. Death awaits!

It was a day of happiness. So much love. We had gone far into the meadow to be alone. Nothing, no one other than ourselves and all the beauty of the world. Her radiance dulled the eternal beauty of the heavens, and I knew I was in love. We walked, just walked. But fate had followed with us.

I left her, just oh so briefly. I had returned to a little place near the village to get some bread and cheese and a little wine. It wasn't far. Just a short walk, a little time apart while I left and returned with the food. Yet it was all the time in the world.

She was to be near a large maple tree in the meadow, waiting for me. A short time apart only. Nothing really. But when I returned, something was wrong. Very very wrong. I approach the place where she is to be waiting. But she is not there. Nowhere in sight. Then! a little ways further into the bush I think I hear a commotion. Yes! a struggle — and a scream.

I drop the basket of food and run toward the area. Anne! Anne! My dear sweet Anne! Let no one harm you or I shall make them pay, I swear I shall!

I burst through the bushes to a small clearing. But a moment too late! An eternity too late! She is here struggling with a stranger, fighting someone. Then! All so quickly, out of nowhere. A shot! A single loud blast from a small musket. And I see the man go down. Limp. Dead. Anne is frozen for the moment, her face aghast with the frenzy of the struggle, and the realization of what has just occurred.

I reach out for her and grab her. The musket falls into the grass. She is pale with terror and a knowledge which I am slow to understand. We hear shouts from beyond the trees. Men are hollering and running in our direction. Footfalls, approaching furiously. And then I see! Oh my God I see and my heart freezes with the terror of the moment. She has killed the son of our King! The prince is dead! He is slain!

I grab her and push her toward the forest. We must run! Leave everything. Run! But the soldiers are close behind us. They are upon the scene immediately. Shouts of "Assassins, assassins — stop them! The prince is dead!" echoes and and reverberates through every fibre of my being and that once beautiful forest glade.

We run and make good our escape. But our world has been shorn to threads, and the hunt for the killers of the King's son is on.

So am I guilty, or am I not? Well, this hardly matters now, for here I am, torn, broken and beaten as I await death.

The executioner lifts the heavy iron bar. Suddenly, a hush falls upon the crowd. I am scared, my God, so scared. In a moment he will bring the bar crashing down upon an arm or a leg — smashing the bone as he moves on to break another limb.

I am trembling now, but very softly I begin to pray. I can hardly formulate the words or thoughts of prayer I am so terrified and frightened. I begin to weep and in a moment I am sobbing like a child. What I wouldn't give for a single sweet peaceful yesterday. Oh God, I am so, so scared of this death.

Time extends. There is not a sound to be heard anywhere lest for my sobbing. I wish I could prepare myself, but I cannot. My body is racked with convulsions. I am so alone, and I am so scared.

And then, only then...

The executioner gently kneels beside my head. He has something he wishes to tell me before beginning. Someone has been with me, unseen, unknown. Gently, so gently now he takes a long stretch of cloth and wraps it about my neck. A bribe has been made. Money has changed hands. I am to be spared the agonies of this death. For before he breaks my body, I will be sent to sleep as he tightens the cord around my neck and ceases the breath within me forever.

And now, only now, as he begins this tender act of mercy, does he whisper into my ear that which is the single most beautiful word in the world...

"Anne."

DAMIAN AND THE 1,000–POUND BENCH

Damian, the weight lifter, strained under the enormous pressure of the weight, as he lay — arms extended and supporting the barbell above him — under the bench press.

"Come on, you can do it," encouraged the coach.

Damian grunted. "It's too much," he exclaimed, "lighten it up."

"No way," responded the coach, "we've gone through this before. This is only two pounds heavier than your last lift. Two measly pounds! Now push like your soul depended on it."

Damian strained, teeth clenched, veins protruding, and gave it his all. Every part of him was focused on the weight above him. Then, with a sputter and a sigh, he pushed the weight straight up, held it for a moment, and finally let it slip onto the heavy supports above him.

"Congratulations," said the coach, "I knew you could do it."

Damian's arms fell to his sides. They felt like rubber. "Whew," he exclaimed, "you really know how to push a guy." He felt spent.

"Well," responded the coach, "that's what I'm here for."

The coach walked over to the weight pile and grabbed two more small plates. He casually slipped them onto each end of the barbell above Damian.

"Oh, Hell," said Damian, watching, "now what?"

"Don't worry," said the coach, "that's only two more pounds added to the bar. Your last lift was 998 pounds, just think of that — 998 pounds! That's incredible. So, now, we go for the biggy — the 1,000-pound lift."

Damian never thought it could have ever been possible, and he said as much.

"Well," said the coach, "that's the way we do it, a pound at a time if necessary. You won't believe how much you can lift."

Damian looked at the bar above him, with its heavy ends sagging downwards. Then, he sighed. "I honestly don't know what I'm doing this for," said Damian.

"Sure you do," responded the coach. "Now grab that bar and let's go!"

Damian grabbed the bar above him, puckered his lips, and exhaled loudly. One thousand pounds. Incredible. Damian remembered a time when he couldn't even lift one hundred pounds.

Damian focused every fibre of his being on the weight above him. All the muscles in his arms and chest tightened as he exerted pressure on the bar and squeezed, arms extended, straight up. So far so good. But now to bring it down to his chest.

"Don't let me down, now," chided the coach, "you can do this."

Damian slowly brought the weight downwards to the point where it was touching his chest. Now came the hard part: pushing it straight up again.

Damian clenched his teeth and held his breath. He squeezed with everything he had, muscles straining, until he was turning purple.

"Exhale, exhale," hollered the coach, "you're holding your breath!"

Damian slowly exhaled and pushed the bar straight up above him — all 1,000 pounds of it. He held the weight for a moment, then let it drop onto the holding brackets.

"Hey, hey!" exclaimed the coach.

"Wow," spurted Damian, "I can't believe it — 1,000 pounds!" Damian sat up to stretch and flex his arms.

"Hey," said the coach, "get back down there, we're not done yet, not by a long shot."

The coach casually slipped two more single-pound plates onto each end of the barbell.

"Yikes," remarked Damian, "and now?"

"Well," responded the coach, "you've made it to the big 1,000, and I'm very proud of you. So now we set our sights on a whole new target — a whole new threshold: 10,000 pounds." The coach was very casual about it.

"10,000 pounds!" shrieked Damian, "10,000 pounds! Are you crazy? Do you know how much 10,000 pounds is! No one can lift 10,000 pounds!"

"Well," responded the coach, in a very laid-back manner, "you're probably right, but after all, we are here for goal-setting, and anyway, we'll just do it one pound at a time if necessary."

"Cripe," protested Damian, "it'll take me to the end of time at least, and then some! 10,000 pounds!"

"Perhaps," came the response, "but then, we do

have to the end of time. In fact, dear one," grinned *he,* "we have to the end of eternity itself. Now, let's proceed, shall we?"

And the coach smiled his wry, wicked smile as only The Devil himself could smile.

THE DECEPTION OF FLIGHT 427

The crew could have been exhausted, burned out, or fed up. But in fact they were simply jacked with the excitement, the relief, the pride and all those other mixed emotions that would accompany such men in such circumstances in this part of history. For they had served their country, the world, and freedom well. They had fought well. And for the over three years they had flown together, they had survived. That was significant. With the world in tatters and desperately trying to find itself, rebuild itself, men such as these could have simply declared that they had done their part, and now wanted to return to their lives: to take time out. But these were no such men. And this was no such time. This was 1946.

It was a large crew. By that in itself it was amazing they were still intact. What are the odds of such a thing? A total of 12 men, they had been splintered many times to fly scores of missions in smaller groups. Yet fate and command always pulled them back together to work their magic collectively. The Battle of Britain. Midnight bombing runs over Germany. Combat runs over the Sea of Japan and the Mediterranean. All had seen action and plenty of it. And each one made it. Survived. But now it was all behind them. Still, they remained a tight crew.

Where so many returned to former lives after the war, this troop was in for life. The service was what made them function, and they were after all, the best of the best. Men such as these were not pushed into civilian lives; not after their sterling records of service and mission accomplishments, and certainly not by the very military that employed them, needed them. The powers that be had need for such fliers, even if there was no longer a war to be waged.

So with that phase of history now over, these 12 members of the United States Army Air Force were being reassigned. No secrecy haunted the new assignment. No warnings or words of caution came down. No hesitations loomed. There was no reason to treat this other than what it seemed to be: a low-priority mission involving the transportation of cargo from halfway around the world and back to the United States. They would be little more than delivery boys on this run. A rather insignificant duty which paled in comparison to some of the daring deeds the crew had flown in recent years. Yet someone somewhere must have known differently. And yes, it was curious that the entire crew was being sent with the full extent of three entire flying fortresses. But such was the decision of the military machine and its mission commanders. These were soldiers, airmen, and they followed orders. The assignment was given the unassuming and rather mundane call sign of Flight Mission 427.

A cargo mission. That was all. Yet it would take them to a portion of the world where none had ever been during or at any time before the war: a little cluster of islands east of the greater land mass of South America — the Falkland Islands. They would depart from the air base in California and then fly southeast high above the coastal waters to an air base outside Tegucigalpa in the Honduras. There they would refuel and continue across the great land mass of Colombia and Brazil to stop yet again for more refuelling at Comodoro Rivadavia in Argentina. And then they would fly straight to their destination: the air base at Stanley on the east Falkland.

It would all be very uneventful. By the clock, by the book. Yet by the time they put down at Stanley, one could not help notice — something? A mood, a manner: something almost intangible with the staffers and cargo crew at the air base. Sombre, tense, hesitant, even cautious. But why? No, such as this seemed to be, it must have been imagined by the team of tired fliers who would stop over for a night and a day before returning with the cargo to the air base in Nevada. And that would be it. This short mission would be over. Still, one of the men had remarked that it gave him... how did Fontaine put it? Pause, concern.

Morning of the second day, and time to depart. Colonel USAAF R.T. Rickman had his men fall in. Flight plans were repeated within the orders, which everyone knew regardless. They would fly straight to Porto Alegre in the southernmost part of Brazil. Here, they would fuel, check the status of the cargo as a matter of standard operating procedure, and then prepare to cross that great mass of unknown territory of this southern continent while heading toward a final refuelling stop in Venezuela. Then, it would be straight home to Nevada.

Time to load. Time to fly. It could have been an omen, it could have been nothing. It happened when Second Lieutenant Wright climbed the metal steps to one of the three Boeing B-17 Flying Fortresses with Waffle, the troop's mascot. Waffle — a Russian Blue male who had been named after the pounding the Luftwaffe suffered at the hands of the Allies — was an exception to operating standards to which the colonel turned a blind eye. But Waffle was still a part of the team. As Second Lieutenant Wright proceeded to board the aircraft with the three year old feline huddled halfway under his jacket, the blue became electrified with anxiety, or terror, or something. It frantically attempted to scamper away, despite Wright's tight hold. This mascot was not new to flying, not by any means. Wright soothed the little beast as best as possible, but it was one of the very few times that any of the men had heard it make that incessant guttural moan, at least not since July of '44 when it came face to face with two captured German fliers.

But, after all, it was just a cat. And despite the looks each of the men shared, none of them really gave it much thought afterward.

A cargo check. The loading had been done in its entirety by the ground crew at Stanley. So, in fact, none of Rickman's crew had seen the load yet. Unusual? Perhaps, but not exactly uncommon. No room for any real alarm here. Each group of four men would take a gander at the cargo on each of the three aircraft. And there they were — canisters: large, black, conspicuous, vague, sinister. Sealed metal drums. Each were quite large, about 200 gallons apiece. Each carried mysterious sequential codings: XE-34-01, XE-34-02, XE-34-03... right up to XE-34-12. A total of 12 containers, four per plane — the same number as the men aboard each aircraft. Just a coincidence.

0-Eight hundred thirty hours: time to depart. Everything a go. The cargo was checked and secured. (Odd though, that there were so few canisters per aircraft when one Boeing could have carried the lot.) Weather was clear. Flight checks were complete, aircraft fuelled and ready. Everything by the book. Everything a check. A go.

The flight to Porto Alegre was without incident, almost mundane. They set down at the airfield as per schedule. Nothing to do here other than refuel for the longest jaunt of the mission: the flight across that giant sea of green unchartered jungle and rain forest. Yet, there it was again: that feeling of hesitation, and quiet, by the ground crew who had been assigned to the 427 at the port. Well, perhaps it was nothing. These were different lands. But there was something about the mood of the place...

Takeoff and departure were just as standard. They were now beginning the greatest leg of the journey. And to this day, no complete details of what might of transpired have been determined — or revealed.

The three Boeings had been flying in flank formation for several hours. All three aircraft had been in constant radio contact with one another — and with Porto Alegre. It occurred on the third B-17 flying at a distant four o'clock position to the Colonel's lead plane. It could have been electrical, but it sounded like a scream — or a howl. And it emanated from the rear of the great aircraft: the cargo area. There is no clear indication of what really went wrong from that point. Despite the Colonel's desperate calls and orders for the third Boeing to respond, there had been clear indication of panic from the pilot. Something was — how did Diller put it? — loose at the rear of the aircraft. Then the Colonel caught what he thought was the sound of a muffled scream, or a gasp, as if of utter astonishment from the pilot. Then, silence.

No sooner had the radio gone cold than the third great Boeing went into a steep pitch. From what the others could see, all four engines seemed to be completely operational on her. Yet, she was now diving at a steep angle nose ward. The Colonel hollered into his radio, begging for response, ordering the crew to bail. Within seconds the aircraft was clearly out of control. No response came back over the radio. There were no indications of anyone aboard trying to react to the emergency. From 10,500 feet, Diller, Lewark, Newkirk and Charlemaigne dove and crashed to their deaths into the jungle far below. No one had bailed. Why? What could have happened? All those men had been in extremely tight situations before. All would have kept their heads regardless of any given emergency aboard their aircraft. Yet all four had gone down for no apparent reason. What on Earth had happened aboard that plane?

The Colonel was on the radio to Porto Alegre immediately. The remaining two Boeings were not capable of setting down in that inhospitable jungle to search for survivors. A rescue would have to be mounted. But suddenly there seemed to be a greater mystery; something beyond the workings of a mere military cargo flight. For the acting commanding officer at Porto Alegre ordered the Colonel and the two remaining aircraft to proceed on their course without hesitation. Ordered! And what of the third Boeing? And her cargo? And those men? The CO simply repeated the order before snapping off the air.

What now? The Colonel would obey his orders. The two remaining B-17s continued on course. Again the Colonel tried to confirm that a search-and-rescue team would be sent out, but the question was side-stepped, avoided. Instead, orders came through for the two B-17s to drop their altitudes to 2,800 feet and reduce air speeds. Twenty-eight hundred?! From 10,500? But why? No reason was given for this. Still, the two Boeing B-17 Flying Fortresses complied and took down their flight altitudes to 2,800 and reduced air speeds.

Hours into the flight after that tragic loss. Near tedium except for the many questions that loomed. It was somewhere over the Mato Grosso that that wild call came in from Lieutenant-Colonel Murdoch who piloted the second Boeing. A commotion had started somewhere in the rear of the aircraft, again — near the cargo hold. It was followed by an inhuman scream, and a highly noxious odor: like ammonia and sulphur. But something was definitely thrashing about wildly at the rear of the plane. Tension ran high. Murdoch sent Second Lieutenant Kessler and Warrant Officer Strom to investigate. Within moments came another scream, this one did sound human. Then, the sound of small-arms fire and what sounded like Kessler shouting over the sounds of more small-arms fire and a frantic, high pitched wail. Finally, complete silence. The potent smell of ammonia and sulphur now wafted through the entire aircraft into the cockpit. In that moment before Lieutenant Murdoch and Major Petri began hollering into their headsets, the Colonel heard what he thought sounded like a flurry of — what? He couldn't tell. Murdoch barely got off what sounded like a warning to the Colonel before everything went dead silent. And then, the second great Boeing B-17 went into a dive and ended somewhere in the jungle near Teles Pires. But Murdoch had managed to get part of his message to the Colonel, something about being in grave danger from the cargo. Then the plane went down.

The Colonel wasn't going to wait. He began screaming into the radio demanding to speak to the CO from Porto Alegre. But the CO wasn't there to respond; or perhaps he wasn't picking up the transmission.

Status: two planes out of three were now down and eight men were likely dead. Before communications went dead with the second aircraft, its pilot had gotten off a frantic word of warning that the third Boeing was also in danger. God knew what that cargo was. It was all highly classified despite its surprising lack of security. But something must have been dangerous enough to have taken down two of the massive Boeing B-17 Flying Fortresses and eight highly experienced airmen.

No response came from Porto Alegre. At least not yet, but the Colonel had no time to hesitate. He ordered co-pilot Captain DeGras and Master Sergeant Heath to suit up and go to the cargo hold and start pitching out the mysterious canisters. Then, the Colonel began an ascent upward in his great Boeing. He wanted to be ready, to cover his bases. If they were in danger and his crew had to bail, he had to be prepared for that. But the current 2,800-foot altitude was too low for such an extreme. So he began the climb, aiming for no less than 7,000 feet but hoping for 10,000 — should it come to that.

Was time of the essence? Unknown. Each of the previous two Boeings had gone down without warning. Something happened aboard them in such short time that not one of eight men had a chance to bail. And then there was that warning from Murdoch...

Up to 4,200 feet, and climbing. DeGras, Heath, and Spencer were now at the rear moving the canisters to the doorway for the drop. Then! Was it Heath who hollered first or Spencer? Something about a strong smell of ammonia — and sulphur — emanating from the canisters. And, my God, did something move within that damn drum? No time to waste. Move! Drop those goddamn things now!

Forty-eight hundred feet and climbing. The drums were heavy, but one was now dropped. Then the real commotion hit. Something is alive in those drums, and it's thrashing about wildly. Then a stronger smell of ammonia and sulphur — and a scream! The Colonel couldn't tell who the scream came from — or what. And he wouldn't have seen the horror that filled DeGras's and Heath's eyes as the three men were about to pitch the second canister. Moments before dropping the second drum, a dark presence broke free. It ripped Spencer's body in half before disappearing out the void with a portion of the dead man's body.

Enough! Forget the two remaining drums. Bail! Bail! Bail! The Colonel caught a glimpse of the altimeter before putting the aircraft to auto and racing for the doorway himself: 5,200 feet. He couldn't tell for certain, but it looked like DeGras and Heath managed to get out successfully before he saw his aircraft for the last time.

★ ★ ★

Today there are rumours. Just rumours. Nothing official has ever been revealed. But there are some reports from within that Colonel Rickman, Captain

DeGras and Master Sergeant Heath did survive the bail-out into the jungle. The Boeing B-17 went down several miles to the north-northeast.

Each of the three airmen were expert survivalists. They would have known how to fend for themselves in the Brazilian rain forest. But you will find no record of their fates, nor that of any search-and-rescue operation, nor any documentation of the cargo that allegedly brought them down.

There are those who will tell you they were all part of the experiment, and its cover-up. Some will tell you that the army sent in one of their special forensic teams and biologic containment units after the planes went down. Then there are those who claim there is no mystery, no cover-up, that all the rumours circulating around Flight 427 are nothing more than overblown ramblings of excitement-craving imaginations. Others claim that those men entered into a desperate run for their lives before they even took off on that fateful mission.

And, there are those who claim they are running still.

THE DAIMONS OF SUFFOLK COUNTY

There is a lamp on the table. It casts only the feeblest light into the room. The walls are dark, the shadows long, the air stale. My head is pounding. A migraine no doubt, perhaps from the red wine, the chocolate, and an abundance of cheap cigar smoke. Honest to God it feels like my forehead is in a vice, with some wretched little demon forever tightening the screws. I might retch if I hadn't emptied myself already. Such misery. Odd how our hopes and dreams are affected by a single moment of pain. It hurts so bad I can barely move. Someone outside is playing that damned macarena: a tune I hate, absolutely loathe. Such a bitter contrast to last night, with the laughter, the dancing... and the love.

Christ. I sound pathetic. A man such as I and almost crippled by this pain, and other things. Worse things. They say the soul can be broken. Well, I hope never to find out, but it's probably not a thing most of us go looking for. Better to wait and just let it happen. But then you've got to be ready.

It's still night. Early, very early. 3:53 according to the digital. Who in the hell would be playing that damned music at this hour? Cool air coming in from the open window now. Feels good. Always been a fiend for it. Night air has a way of snapping me back to reality, back to earth. It stimulates so many senses. I smell it, feel it. God, I swear I can even taste it. Remembrances of blessed creation in the subtlest of forms. Such poetry. But then, not all things flow. Especially of late, I have to wonder: where's the rhyme?

Things are definitely feeling out of sync. Like the conversation last night, strange. And the people, and other things: all somehow different, odd. Daimons.

Yeah. We were whirling around the dance floor. What a time. I haven't heard so much waltz and rumba since I was a kid. Great moments. Very nice. Linda was heaven, as always. Such a beautiful woman: charming, elegant, refined, and always a little naughty. What a knock-out in a black evening dress. No one there would have suspected her sportier side. Or the other things. Thank God. But that's all behind us now.

Maybe some of the punch got to me. I know better than to drink the stuff, but when it's there in front of you and you're whooping it up, it's hard to say no. One small glass is all it takes. Bad idea following it up with the wine. We live but we never learn. That's the way of parties though, letting loose. Too bad for the results.

The chandeliers stay in mind. Such huge and magnificent things. They each looked like they weighed a ton. A nightmare keeping all that glass and crystal so clean, I'm sure. It's mesmerizing watching those lights dance and flicker. Like little — what? You know I want to say it: like little somethings with minds and wills of their own. Radiant. But maybe not so pure.

They did dance around, didn't they? Flowing, moving mysteriously. But not so freely. No. Some kind of order, some kind of purpose. It was likely my objectivity that kept me focused, in touch with myself. But not Linda. She was right in the midst of it, totally ensconced. I have to admit, I don't recall it all. I can't even be sure I know where memory and imagination meet on this one. If I were any other man I might write it off to the alcohol, or the results of the migraine. But I'm too stable to let booze affect me like that. So I have to wonder.

The scene unfolds. Quite surreal. She was passed out, I'm sure of it. But not from liquor, that's the funny thing: she doesn't drink. A teetotaler. Linda's never needed it. She's upbeat and giddy enough without that crutch. Still, she was flat out. I'm certain of it.

So when and how? Hard to retrace the steps. She was full of life all night. And such a dancer. Good orchestra now that I recall. Our kind of music, not like the stuff they play nowadays. Wonderful strings: very clear, so resonant in that big hall. The high tones kept ringing in our ears long after we'd left. Well, something was ringing. Like when you leave a rock concert and your ears just vibrate for hours and days on end afterward. Something was still sounding in my mind much later. No question about that. But in retrospect... I'd have to think: not like an instrument. Just a tone, or a layering of tones. Electronic maybe. Can't quite pin it down. Perhaps a bit like tinnitus — when a phantom pitch affects your hearing but you know there's no sound. Except there was sound, I'm sure of it. If nowhere else then at least in our minds.

Harlan was quite the joker. At times I can barely

stand the guy, but he maintained his charade without the usual boorish overtones. Amazing how people can become the clothes they're wearing. The tuxedo actually seemed to suit him: his personality that is. Another person with the gift of gab, always something to say. Not like me: too thoughtful and honest to let words just flow out of me, betray me. It was interesting conversation though, I have to admit. People love to reminisce. But then they tend to recall memories with a greater fondness than is due. Or the memories change and they find themselves slobbering over what never happened or never mattered anyway. Or did it? It depends on the person. Last night was the case in point.

Linda and I go a long way back: to when we were kids. She's never been the type to exaggerate things — quite the opposite, she understates. I've known her long enough to know. When she gets talking about things past, there's little room for doubt. She just doesn't so much as play on imagination. But her understated recollections leave plenty of room for interpretation: for filling in the blanks. What she doesn't say can reveal a lot, and leave even bigger questions.

Like those experiences of hers: the ones she claims to have had way back. Why would she lie? She wouldn't. Especially 25 years after the fact. People just don't hang on to fibs they might have created when they were nine years old. It simply doesn't happen. And to see her face when she talks about it.

God. You know something has affected her deeply. What's worse, you realize there's a lot there that she probably doesn't even remember — or know — or want to know.

She was raised near the woods so she'd be familiar with the many explanations for those early memories: that one late afternoon of feeling vulnerable while out walking, then helpless, very helpless. Intermittent memories of large dark eyes — like a deer's, she'll always say. When she talks about it, you know that something was happening, something she can never recall — with someone or something there, controlling, governing. It's very eerie. But it's the tone of her voice that gets me every time — and the way her eyes occasionally well up when she tries to remember.

That's where the talk went last night. That topic. It's the one thing that'll make Harlan absolutely grave, morose. Knocks the wind right out of him every time. He's even worse than Linda when the conversation starts. I guess when something really strikes home it can break through phony put-ons every time. It's weird. You know he wants to talk about it, open up, but then something inside him always makes him clam up; like there's some little battle going on within him. You can see the character of the man change right there before your eyes. The talk rambles, then dies, and then things get completely quiet. That's when you realize something has happened. But I'm not the type to push. Better to leave some things alone.

That's partly the reason I suggested we leave when we did, Linda and I that is. Well, I'm pretty sure I'm the one who made the suggestion, but what does that matter? The point is, the two of us finally decided to go, to get away from a mood that became sombre. It was getting late anyway. She had become quiet, and as for me, I had had enough noise for one evening. So we left together. It was a beautiful night too. We got into the car and decided to drive for a while. You know, just get away and breathe the night air. It was nice. We were on the outskirts as it was, so we just kept heading into the country — where you could smell the spruce and be completely away from the lights and noise.

We lapped up the highway. Linda was grand to behold. Too bad the car wasn't a convertible, but we made do. We had the windows all the way down so she could let her head tilt part way out and have the wind blow through her hair. She looked so serene. It brought back more memories: the kind that bring a touch of sadness because you know things could have been different. Younger days.

It all seemed a lifetime ago: what we had and what we lost. Funny how fate puts certain people together. But then we blow it anyway. Like us. We pretty much grew up together, and a bond developed that was greater than mere friendship. By high school, we were tight — an item, destined to reach the stars together. But when you're so young, what do you know about such things? I wanted to go out and conquer the world, with little thought of what I had. How sad. How typical. I left, travelling, moving around, working: being the grand adventurer, having experiences: things I would one day write about. Meanwhile, the greatest thing in my life was left alone, abandoned. I didn't return for over 10 years. We barely stayed in touch. My fault again. By the time I came home, things had changed. Really changed. That's when it hit me that I had it all — and lost it. Now when we're together, I think both our hearts can't help but feel broken for the things that should have been. That's the pain of it: knowing now that I loved her but was too blind to see it.

Meanwhile, through all that, she was busy having some experiences of her own. Not the kind people go out looking for either. Still, I'd say she held up well. At least from what I've heard. Over time, the rumours couldn't help but get out. That's human nature, I suppose. It is interesting what people imagine, or find out. Much of it is usually based on truth. Like those little pinhead-sized scars of hers, and the periods of missing time that preceded their appearance. I'm one of the few people she's ever shown them to. The first time I saw them, it sent a chill right through me, I have to admit. They looked innocent, but not natural — like incisions. They took forever to heal too. She had them checked, but the doctors couldn't figure them out. And Linda's not diabetic, in fact she's very healthy, so why would they not heal? Then there's her trying to remember where they came from. That's when she finds herself staring into the void, with nothing other than big dark eyes staring back — deer's eyes.

There was stranger stuff. Like the period when she stopped menstruating and began gaining weight. Obvious, except she hadn't been with anybody. Nobody. After a couple of months it just suddenly stopped, and her weight returned to normal. And again — nothing but memories of the blackness. She started to panic. Who wouldn't? But she held up. It's amazing the way she just keeps this all bottled in. Hard to know how someone could cope with such stuff. She's a strong lady.

A mystery, but still — someone I've always loved. We didn't speak a lot in the car. All the talking had been done at the party. This was the quiet time, the escape for two distinctly different people who could appreciate each other's idiosyncrasies. So we let the ride and the highway speak to us in our own personal way. We just kept going.

We ended up on a winding road that wasn't familiar. We just followed it, letting it guide us. Other lights passed us, but we paid no attention. I heard what sounded like the scream of a hawk, but hawks don't hunt at night, so I don't know what it was. The air was definitely getting cooler. She seemed okay with it.

A crystal-clear night, doubtless from the cool air. Stars galore. And me, still reeling from the effects of all that alcohol. Finally, having to pull over and get out. You know — that phase when the booze starts to wear off and leaves you feeling a bit unsettled. That's when my head pain kicked in. I'm sure it was triggered by all the headlights.

Some kind of pain shot through my head. It happened quite suddenly. When you're driving in the black of night your eyes will adjust to the darkness. So it doesn't help when someone comes beetling over the hill with their headlights on full beam. It caught me off guard. But by now we were stopped and I was out of the car.

I was leaning against the hood, taking a few drags on one of the coronas they had passed out at the party. Not the best cigar, and probably another dumb move considering the way I was feeling. The car was turned off so it was pretty quiet. But we were still getting bathed in passing lights. They sure were bright.

She was flat out. I don't know where my mind was, I must have been feeling tipsier than when we left: likely from the way the night air was hitting me. I guess I let myself go a bit. Vertigo. Now the stars were dancing around. Some party.

I think Harlan was there. Haven't I covered this? I'm getting confused about the sequence of events. That's just the way migraines affect me. He didn't seem himself. He was dazed, completely elsewhere: probably the booze. Linda must have been dog-tired, no other reason for her to be passed out like that. But I was too into myself at the time to give it any real thought.

The surrounding trees took on a life of their own. Again, the booze. Some insight into what it must be like to be schizophrenic: like we were being watched from the bushes, or elsewhere. Eyes. Nocturnal ones, and my crazy imagination. We did see something... a buck, or an owl; something looking our way.

When did she get out of the car? I barely remember. Harlan was behaving like an automaton: a good little soldier, not himself. Strange. They just weren't acting normal. Too compliant — manipulated, like people without wills of their own. And me with the head pain, just wishing those damned lights weren't so bright. Then, far away from the car — a mirage — or something. Blues. Greys. Colours that didn't fit the terrain.

The migraine, of course. People can't function with them. Everything was exploding inside my head with the light — and the noise: a cacophony of sound; resurgences of the orchestra. Huge. Awesome the way it emitted such chaotic noise; all brought together with such fine resolution; harmoniously, purposefully. I don't think she was aware of it the way I was. I don't think either of them were.

There was a moment of some intensity. I don't know what it was or why I would think it. Probably nothing, just me. I'm reading into this. I know things got quiet. After all, it was the dead of night.

Then what? I don't know. That's what's so embarrassing, I just can't remember, I don't even recall the ride back into town. All I know is I'm here, flat on my back. I trust the car is outside, it must be. I'll check in the morning. I just don't remember making the drive back, but how else would I be here?

Someone has finally turned off that damned music outside. Quiet, finally. Maybe my headache will start to break now. I need rest, real sleep. I think I'll turn off the lamp; let the darkness embrace me. Funny, I hadn't even noticed the ceiling fan until now, moving so slowly, spinning...

Oh the hell with it. I've just overdone it. I'll know better for the next time. Chalk it up to another experience of overkill. Parties, they can be the life and death of us. I hope Linda and Harlan are okay. I wonder if I'll ever get to see them again.

RAIDERS OF THE WORLD

Langston tossed fitfully, and then, quite suddenly, he was awake. There he was, in his real little world; lying on his futon, the radio playing, the sounds of streetcars and motor traffic outside the balcony of his second-floor bachelor pad. Another reckless night. Stupid. It could really be a hassle sometimes: tossing and turning all night long, and it wasn't exactly visions of sugar plums dancing through his head that kept him bouncing in and out of the world of dreams. These weren't any childlike cascades or enticing landscapes of peaceful meadows. Nothing of the sort. He rose and quickly realized he had the makings of a headache. Another friggin' headache. Great. Nothing completely unusual here either: just part of the package deal that came with the restless night. He popped a couple of AC&C's and got coffee going in the percolator. Extra strong coffee. Better to deal with the headache now before it reached full blossom and really threw a wrench into his day. (That was something he had learned from much experience. The headaches never went away on their own. Never. Even if he took aspirins later in the morning, they always just got worse. The trick was to kill the suckers while the hint of their presence was first felt.) Langston thanked God for painkillers. And the pharmaceutical companies should thank God for the likes of over-the-counter consumers like Langston.

He stepped through the open door onto the balcony. Five-thirty a.m. and a Saturday. Good grief.

Earlier than sanity should permit and the first day of the weekend. At least it was summer and the makings of a beautiful day. Blissful reality. Nothing like what was in that last dream of his. He shivered from the fragmented memory of it. He meandered a bit while overlooking the busying street below, waiting for the coffee. Things seemed so placid and peaceful on the street; like a modern day fairy tale. He liked it. Summer should be here all year 'round — and the blue sky, and the windless days, and the sounds of young families. Compared to those dreams, it was grand.

The coffee. It was strong all right. Lately he'd really gone into a phase of seeking stronger and stronger brews. Even the two coffee houses downtown had gotten to know him as a challenge to satiate his needs for dark and malevolent roasts. They always joked with him about that. But right now he sat on the five dollar lawn chair of his balcony with brew in hand and sipped. Finally, the headache blissfully disappeared along with the sensations and memories of the night before. Complete consciousness now started to finally and truly kick in. Whew.

They didn't know what they had latched onto. The beacon had strayed wildly trying to find its mark, actually — one of many, countless marks. Then, something seemed to connect. There was a feeling of excitement — and hope. Suddenly they became eager. Certain receptors could be wide open — open to almost anything. And now, the Highers, the True Controllers, could feel it too.

A connection. Feelings of blissful achievement welled up. It might be cause for celebration. They homed in and concentrated, focused. This could be it. This really could be IT.

She was talking nonsensically, rambling — and with an increasing sense of urgency. Trying to get a warning out. Yet everything seemed like a fog: chaos. She just couldn't seem to focus or collect herself. Hysteria? She'd never been prone to it before. Not ever. Not after growing up on the farm and having seen various forms of labour related accidents and not as one of the youngest women cadets ever to qualify for flight school. Even on that one night 11 months back in a rare night dive when she'd briefly lost consciousness, she was still in control when she came to. But this was different. This was like being covered in a heavy blanket of tar while you waited for the napalm to ignite. And this time, someone she loved very much was involved. And the danger was so damned real — but elusive. Damn it! She fought to get her bearings and now discovered her body wouldn't respond. Gas? When could they have hit? She summoned all her strength to get out her one warning. Then, in a microsecond she thought she got a glimpse of something: something that took its own moment to connect with the very core of her being, something that really did scare her. There was a pause as if creation itself had ceased. A lull. Absolute nothing. Then, she saw... *it*. Now the scream did come; a scream that emanated right from the bowels of her soul and rang-up to the height of the rafters. Then, blissfully, she woke up — and retched.

But she collected herself. A dream. Geeze. She'd been through all the psych routines and analyses of various post traumatic stress disorders, but this was a doozey. She covered the spot where she'd brought-up with a few handfuls of straw. Then she really started to come around and took a good look around her. The barn was beautiful. Fresh straw, the tall arched roof, a combination of the scent of clean air and old wood and memories of years upon years of hide-'n-seek and horses and... Well, of course, no one else would see it quite the way she did, but then no one else had her recollections of this place or of catching mid-day catnaps in the straw like she had done just now. In any other case, if she or anyone else had let out a scream like that last one, you could be sure that dad or Aunt Mae or someone would come running right soon. But for now they had all gone for the afternoon to the enjoy the festivities of the local rodeo. That was the deal. They would all go and leave Jessica alone to rest and reminisce as part of her three-day leave. So much for peaceful mid-afternoon catnaps in the straw.

Almost! Just a little bit closer next time. This one almost came through. The connection was made all right, but it got loose somehow, slipped away. Perhaps a better effort was needed: more focus, better concentration. Someone just wasn't paying enough attention, wasn't doing their bit. And this was being monitored! Tested!

Better find that pitfall and remedy it for the next time — if there was a next time. Got to keep trying, pressing on. If this happened again, the Highers could start getting upset. Then they might want to step in; to take control. And nobody wanted that. Absolutely nobody but nobody wanted THAT!

Emma was getting old. Well, that was hardly debatable. She was old. At 89 it wasn't as if she had a lot of years ahead of her. Some people could make it to her age, mind you, and seem as sprightly and young as if they had another 20 years left in them. But not Emma. Her clock was definitely ticking. Her day consisted of little more than watching TV, or listening to the local high school drama class read excerpts of Shakespeare, or just nodding off in her wheelchair right after feeding time. Such is the way of old age. And one thing the experience of old age eventually teaches each and every one of us, it has this curious way of letting you thrive in the land of memories; real or imagined. That's what kept Emma so blissfully happy, despite the wheelchair and that acrid smell of stale urine and ammonia — memories. God bless 'em. And memories were what filled Emma's old and fragile mind just before she starting drifting away again into that blissful, peaceful land of sleep...

Bingo! This one we got. But watch that over-confidence boys. It's like they say: focus, focus, focus. First you gotta snag 'em, then comes the tough part: reeling them in. Well, it's not like it's exactly easy. Especially with these oldies. They're always ripe and ready for the experience, until it comes to those damned fragile minds of theirs. It's always the same: baiting and hooking them comes well enough, but when it gets time to securing them and taking over, that's when they always tend to pop off. Poof! Dead as doornails. But this one we got. This one we got...

Jerry and Lyle had just come in from another exhausting half weekend with their dad. It was always the same: every time he picked them up for their time together, he'd planned so many things for them to do together that by Sunday afternoon the two 12 year-olds were completely wasted. Spent. Kaput. First, they went out Saturday morning for a big brunch. They stuffed themselves, and then they just talked and talked and talked. Then it was off to a movie matinee. A good one too. After that they were just in time to make it to that baseball game. Hot dogs, popcorn, and a beer for dad. Then, back to his place where he made supper for the lot of them and finally, they spent the evening playing video games and doing more talking. Sunday morning they were all up early for a hike outside the city, then another meal. It was a very fun packed busy two days. And what the hell? It was just a dad loving his sons and trying to show them a good time. So by the time they got back to mom's, the two exhausted youths both headed straight to their rooms to crash. Off came the sneakers and down went the heads as each one slipped into the world of sleep, and deep deep dreams...

Yee-hah! A couple more. A whirl of excitement welled up throughout the organization and moods began to soar.

Sometimes things just fell into place so beautifully, as if it was all part of the grand scheme of things. A few of the supervisors had their look-see and confirmed that everything was proceeding to plan. Yup. Couldn't be better. This could really be it. Somebody call head office and tell the boys in C Section to get ready. We're finally gonna do it. Everyone take your positions and inform your staff, we're getting ready to move...

It must have been, quite simply, that her time was up. Certainly, she had lived a good long life, but all things must come to an end. She never even woke from her gentle little nap. If someone had been watching her though, they might have detected that single moment when something went wrong. It was a brief little period when — deep in her sleep — something seemed to startle her, caught her right off guard. Her frail little chest rose ever so slightly, and then — she was gone. Emma was dead. And with her died her dreams.

Two little boys were being roused from blissful afternoon naps. It began with a booming racket. Then, it seemed to transform itself into someone's voice — a familiar voice — calling out in a strange but familiar landscape. Then, together, quite suddenly, they were awake — and mom was at their side telling them to get ready for supper. She had just made their favourite dish, lasagna. But first, time to wash, then head downstairs to eat.

And around the world, a multitude of sleepers, nappers and dozers experienced a "blip" of disturbance deep within their dreams that none would ever remember. Nor would anyone have known about the fallout from that single minute portion of disturbance which occurred *elsewhere...*

Hey! It's gone! What the hell happened? We were locked on, we had it. Then what? Nothing. In fact, we had a bunch of 'em lined up. Now we're back at zero. Zilch. We're... WHAT? Oh no! — not THAT! We've been SHUT DOWN? — AGAIN?!! The last time THAT happened it took almost 1,500 years to resolve! Don't they realize it's all the same basket of eggs? Does the chief executive understand the seriousness of this? We almost had it, for crying out loud. Now who knows how long it'll be before we're up and running again. This is nuts — it'll be back to the drawing board for who knows how long!

Work shutdowns and our union — they'll be the death of us yet.

THE MANIFEST

Would we rather believe that it never happened? That it never came? Wouldn't we all. Yet, it is worth remembering, even reliving, so that we might all come to understand what it was. But then we must be sure that we never forget. For as with all history, we are doomed to repeat what we do not learn. This one time, we must learn. We absolutely must learn.

It must have seemed like a land of chaos to it — our planet Earth. A not-altogether old world, but one that sprouted life and developed rather abruptly in the overall age of the cosmos. By the time man first appeared, our infesting little species had progressed quickly — seemingly overnight. And although man had grown quickly, he had not *advanced,* and therein lay the beginnings of our doom. We must have caught its notice while heading toward 5.5 billion strong. With such numbers came the many problematic scenarios that would have attracted it. Fed it. Perhaps it simply waited. Perhaps it knew us better than we knew ourselves. If there is competition in the universe for water, food, or air, it was none of these that brought it. More than 70 per cent of the Earth is covered in water, but it came for not so much as a drop to drink. Nor did it come for our forests, our oxygen, nor even for the planet itself. It came to feed.

I am a drifter. Though not the kind you might associate with misgivings about tardiness or predispositions towards unruliness. I simply drift. Life is far too short for me to be anything other than its watcher. I live for the moment and for the next awakening day. But I am a man of virtue and my word. I do not lie. I do not steal. I work a hard honest day and am likely to be as tired at the end of my day as you are at yours. I have seen much of this grand continent. My horse is a well used '79 HD Heritage Softail, and she suits me well. I have worked at many jobs, but I was on a farm when this ghastly and yet wondrous story began. And I will tell you that whatever a lady fate may be, she is full of surprises.

Yet, as I begin the tale, I find myself wondering what really did happen; even if it did happen. For though I have the mind of a healthy skeptic, there are things in this world that simply transcend all common sense and sound judgment. All is not as it seems.

It was the summer of '91 when I ventured out west to Alberta, where I settled outside of Calgary. I had pulled up stakes as a sheet metal worker in Manitoba and simply made the decision to move. I was not desperate for money but, nonetheless, I sought work as soon as I realized it was an area where I wanted to stay. It was a difficult time there, as it was elsewhere in the country. The province had been hit hard by the recent recession. People had gone through major upheavals. Bankruptcies, downsizing and cutbacks all contributed to job loss and economic uncertainty. Many had lost their homes along with their sources of income. Ranching and farming had met their own unique crises, and some families were losing land and a way of life that had been passed down through generations. The mood was somber. Joy was scarce. Dreams had to be put on hold or discarded altogether. The robust moxie of the west had given way to doubt and despair. Still, I was attracted to the land and its people and found that some personal good fortune had followed me.

Ben Gasner brought me on. He was a farmer and rancher with about 1,200 acres of land in the foothills. A kind man of 50, he stood a mere 5'7" but had the strong, sinewy look of his trade — a horseman. Only a slightly thickening midriff gave away his age, for he was both young of mind and spirit. His preference and love was for horses, and his dream was to establish himself as one of the top breeders and horse farmers in the world. But he was a shrewd businessman, and until he could accomplish his goal, the practicality of cattle ranching kept his business running.

Not that I've had much experience with horses or other livestock, at least not to the extent that Ben's ranch required. I do love animals however, and as a young child was exposed to a fair number, mostly domestic, while growing up in northern Quebec. I recall a time when I was eight and visited a second cousin's farm up near Tobermory in Ontario. I was given a chance to try my hand at riding a young Charolais calf. It bucked me right off and stomped on my left toe. That was my first experience with a beef breed. In that same week, I also got to try my hand riding Icelandic ponies. That was a great deal more rewarding, and less painful too.

Ben Gasner's place had Icelandics. In fact, Ben had pretty much of everything, both for breeding as well as for his personal likes. He introduced me to a number of breeds: types that I may have heard about or seen in pictures, but never up close. The majority of his breeds was a selection of fine American Quarter horses and Kentucky Saddlers, which stands to reason from the business perspective. But he also relished lesser knowns: including a half dozen Tobiano Pintos, several Welsh ponies, and even a couple of Pinzgauer Norikers, which suited the ranch well considering their sure-footed abilities in hilly and mountainous regions. My favourite, however, was an East Bulgarian named Kingsley. Kingsley and I quickly became the best of friends, and grew able to read each others mood and manner as horse and rider.

Ben Gasner was also a happily married man — her name was Laura. Having been raised in Calgary, she was as much at home on the ranch as in the city. Laura was almost petite; at 5'5" and weighing no more than 115 pounds she was both feminine and beautiful. She could saddle a mount and ride superbly. Plus, she had recently taken up kick-boxing once a week near the city. Still, she was one of the most graceful women I'd ever met.

By the time I got settled at the ranch, it was the end of June. The Gasners had no children, so besides myself and the occasional drifter, the only other person who was there to help Ben was another loner named Jordan. At 26, Jordan was an expert and gifted horseman. Ben had told me numerous times that if it hadn't been for Jordan, there were periods when the ranch would have been far too much for the couple to handle.

Jordan stayed with the Gasners in their ranch house. I had the benefit of living alone in a small and humble hired-hand house which was laid out like a small one bedroom apartment. It suited me well and was a quiet place to flop after some very exhausting days. On occasion, the lot of us would drive into Calgary for an evening of wining and dining. The city had experienced some phenomenal growth over the previous decade, and had all the hustle and bustle of a larger American city, though on a smaller scale. That was the beauty of Calgary: a city of no more than 750,000 and just 40 minutes away from the ranch and the beautiful foothills of Alberta. Another 30 minutes and you'd find yourself in the middle of some of the most breathtaking mountains on all the Earth. The whole area was like a piece of paradise, and I fell in love with it instantly.

I'm sure it took interest in the area for reasons that were far more tactical. All things considered, the terrain and population of that part of the country could lend itself to its special kind of infection (or dare I say invasion?). Population densities between Calgary and Vancouver are relatively sparse. So from a strategic viewpoint, the city would be seen as the ideal target for the manifestation, or whatever it might have been. From such a source, it could have gained knowledge — and strength — to branch out like a web to the north, the west, and certainly across the border to the south. Plus, there were the open spaces of land like Ben's ranch — and then of course, there were the animals. So that was its point of contact.

It must have been in the first week of July, though I don't remember the date exactly. To call it a strange thing would be the understatement of our lives, for we couldn't possibly have known what we were witnessing. It was simply the beginning. Ben and Jordan and I were on horseback inspecting long stretches of fencing for breaks and damages. Ben was always a man to have the good sense to avoid mishaps with proper preventive maintenance. It was about five in the afternoon on a warm day with the sun just beginning its journey toward the peak of the Rockies. We came over an embankment near a small creek and stopped to let the horses drink. We all heard it together but Jordan spoke first.

"Listen up," Jordan said. "What do you make o' that?" We all sat motionless for a moment.

"Is it electrical?" Ben wondered, " 'cause it sure sounds that way, though there aren't any hydro lines near enough as far as I know."

The sounds were like a high pitched screeching, and Ben was right, it could have been mistaken as electrical. Sad to say though it wasn't.

"Wait a minute," I said. "It's coming from over this direction, come on."

The sounds were roughly to our left and over a

small ridge. We rode up no more than 20 yards and sat — stunned for the moment — staring at the unbelievable scene before us.

And "My God," was all any of us could utter.

There, twisting and writhing on the ground — in broad daylight — were a half dozen raccoons: all in apparent agony. Splotches of blood pooled the area. Each of the animals were hemorrhaging — through their eyes, ears and noses. And they were flipping around in fits of pain as if they were being burned alive. Ben was the first to react.

"Jordan!" Ben blurted. "Your .22!"

Jordan produced his .22 rifle, styled after one of the old fashioned Winchesters, and passed it to Ben. Ben was practically beside himself as he started putting each animal down with a single shot to the head. He was right to do it too, it didn't take the intellect of a surgeon to realize that those animals were in agony. The stench of the area was second only to the cries of their death throes. They couldn't even run once Ben started firing. One by one the high pitched screams were silenced. By the time it was all over, the three of us fell into a numb silence.

"What in God's name could ha' done that?" Ben asked, partly to us and partly to himself. "Was that stream poisoned or infected with something? Did those things drink from the same water our horses just drank from?"

A good question. But all those raccoons drinking from the same creek, at the same time? And during the day? Not likely. It seemed more reasonable to me that something had poisoned the ground or the foliage. But birds and insects in the area seemed okay, and the plants and grass all looked green and healthy. Was it a sound? Did a high-pitched frequency that only an animal might hear cause this? If so, why weren't the horses bothered? Stranger yet, how did all those animals gather in that one spot to suffer from the same thing? We collected two of the dead for Ben's vet to examine. If something was infecting the wildlife in the area, we would have to know about it.

By the time it was nearing 6 p.m. we were back at the house. Ben hollered for Laura but she was nowhere in sight. The Chevy pick-up was gone so she was likely elsewhere on the ranch or out doing errands. Jordan and I sat down on the porch while Ben made a call to a local animal doctor, someone by the name of Colin Lay who had known Ben and his animals for years. Ben explained in explicit detail what we had found. He told Colin he wanted the dead raccoons checked out right away for poisons or infectious diseases. Rabies never really occurred to any of us but Colin brought it up as a feasible cause for the strange deaths.

Ben joined us on the porch and passed us each a Heineken. Ben said he wanted to wait for Laura, even though there was another vehicle by the house we could have used. It wasn't a long wait. Ten minutes later, Laura came driving up to the house. She was covered in dust and bits of sand but still looked stunning with her long auburn hair falling raggedly over her shoulders. After a few short hello's and a brief explanation from Ben the three of us loaded into the Chevy and headed down the highway with the dead animals to see Colin. Laura decided to stay home, despite the mystery at hand.

Colin was a tall and rail-thin man of 42. His silvery grey hair and vandyke set off the most piercing grey blue eyes I've ever seen. Quick and adroit movements revealed a keen and active mind. His place had the putrid smell of ammonia and animal waste. The clinic was a sealed off portion of his house, with a separate entry.

"Find out as quick as you can what they were suffering from," Ben said. "These things were in agony. I've never seen anything like it."

"And there were a total of... what? Six?" Colin asked.

"Yeah, six," Ben answered, "including these two."

"Damn strange to have more than just a couple of these on the same patch of ground at the same time," Colin offered, "especially during the day."

"You're tellin' us," Ben retorted.

"And you said they were... screaming?" Colin asked.

"Never heard nothin' like it," Jordan cut in. "These things were all twisted up, spewin' blood."

"Well, I can't do much right now," Colin said. "Leave them with me overnight and I'll see if I can have some answers for you in the morning."

We departed and filed back into the pick-up. That

night was spent caring for the horses and drinking beer on the porch. This time Laura joined us.

"Why don't you each grab a mount and take them out for a stretch?" Ben taunted.

" 'Cause it's already evenin' ya darn fool," Laura retorted, all the while giving me a wink. "An' besides, who'd be able to keep up with me?"

"Ain't that the truth," Ben chuckled.

"Well," I said. "I guess we'll never know who can keep up with whom!"

Laura gave me her best sideways leer. For someone who didn't talk much, she did have a way of communicating with very few words. We spent the rest of the evening sitting around, making idle chat and watching the stars that shone overhead. But our minds were elsewhere.

The following day started out as any other. We continued with the fencing and got a bit of riding in. Colin got in touch with Ben two days after we saw him: his explanation for the raccoons misery was strange. Colin hadn't found the reason for the pains of the raccoons, but he did say that there seemed to have been extreme stress on their nervous systems, as if they'd been subjected to intense electrical shocks. No rabies. And there was nothing in the area that could have created the conditions Colin was trying to pinpoint. At least, nothing known. But that wasn't the strangest part. The day after we saw Colin, a couple from the city drove to his clinic with two semiconscious wild dogs. Apparently, the dogs were near death when the couple found them by the roadside of the secondary highway to Canmore. They soon died from the same type of stress we witnessed in the raccoons.

"Something odd and grotesque is happening around here," Ben blurted out as we sat around the supper table that evening, "and whatever it is, whether it's something toxic or a disease being transmitted between the animals, we've gotta be darn certain it doesn't reach the horses or the rest of the livestock."

"But Colin must have some idea what it must be," Laura offered.

"If he has," Ben returned, "he's keepin' it to himself, at least he's not tellin' us. In fact, he said he sent both the raccoons and the wild strays to the university for further study."

During the next week, more and more reports were coming in from people discovering animals dead or, finding them as we had, in contortions of pain. Small articles start appearing in each of the Calgary papers. At that point, whatever was killing the animals hadn't crossed the barrier into domestic animals and livestock. That soon changed, not eight or nine days after we first made our discovery.

It was just before 5 a.m. when we were all startled awake by a commotion: A scream, loud and intense, echoed across the field to the house and my living quarters. Ben and Laura were the first outside, Jordan and I followed. What I saw will forever remain with me. Ben went half crazy. It was the horses. Strewn across a portion of a two-acre, fenced in portion of the field were a half dozen Saddlers. We hadn't put them in the livery stable the night before. Now, they were lying in the open field twisting and writhing, baying and gasping in the same fits of anguish and agony we had witnessed before. Whatever had been affecting the smaller mammals had now bridged the gap to the horses. I would never have thought a horse could manage sounds as they made. It was the nearest thing to a human scream imaginable.

We were frantic. The four of us ran toward them, looking for whatever the hellish cause might have been. The sun was just beginning to come over the horizon, but we couldn't see a thing; nothing that might have caused this.

"Goddam it," Ben screamed. "What the hell is doin' this? Someone get Colin on the goddamed phone and tell him to get out here."

I bolted for the house and got on the phone. Colin made his best speed to the ranch, but it was still the longest 15 minutes I've ever waited, watching those horses, not knowing what to do. A horse is an intelligent animal, typically high-strung and with a well-developed nervous system. Knowing this made it almost unbearable for us to watch and listen to those screams. We would have tranquilized them but we didn't have any tranq left. Ben anguished over the idea of putting the horses down with his .303, but Laura and Jordan convinced him to wait.

Finally, Colin arrived with his niece, Shannon, who

couldn't have been more than 13 or 14 years old. She let out a scream herself when she heard the horses. She wouldn't come any closer and chose to stay beside the car. Colin's face was one of disbelief and shock. Despite the fact he'd done some work on the raccoons, nothing had prepared him for this. He tranquilized them right away. Within minutes, the field was silent as the horses fell unconscious, but the sounds still seemed to reverberate in the air and through our own shattered nerves. Shannon stood by the car crying. We were all in tears.

"What in God's name is doing this, Colin? Do you know?" Ben was exasperated.

"I've never seen anything like it," was all Colin could say. "Never."

That was the morning that really marked the beginning. Out of the six horses that lay in the field that day, four died within the hour from their ordeals. One slipped into a coma. The other was kept unconscious while Colin brought it back to his clinic. Things went insane after that.

News made its way to The Herald. A couple of reporters came to speak with Ben, and finally with Colin too. The Sun copied the story, adding their own contrived and sensational hype. The University of Calgary got into the picture, as did the Board of Health, Dept. of Agriculture, the Veterinary Board, and a number of other scientific and medical associations. The cause of the horses' deaths was never determined, or at least, we weren't told much. It wasn't viral, wasn't any form of rabies, nothing toxic could be found in the area, and no human factor was blamed. All that was known was that the horses' nervous systems were subjected to severe stress. In layman's terms, Colin told us, it was as if their pain centres had gone ballistic. The pain was enough to kill them.

News about the event travelled fast. Ranchers and farmers took what precautions they could, but they were fighting an invisible enemy. The Game and Wildlife Association went on alert for what they thought might be a new strain of rabies that had likely developed in the foothills, and which they feared could spread into the national parks as well as outside the province. But other questions loomed.

Why, for example, were just those horses affected? Ben's ranch is home to over two dozen horses and ponies. Why weren't more down? The six were together in the field for the evening. It was almost as if they were selected. But by what? If it was some sort of bug, wouldn't it have spread to the other horses in the nearby stables? And another puzzling question: Ben employs cattle-cutting in his fields, so a number of Holstein-Friesians and Jerseys were nearby. Why weren't the cows affected? Just like the raccoons we had killed, and the stray dogs, there was something very odd occurring: something that did not act like rabies, or a virus, or disease, or even toxic for that matter. Something was in the area that targeted specific animal groups within small areas, and it was selective. Goddam it, it was selective.

By early August, accounts were trickling in of select groups of wild animals and livestock in a growing 50-mile radius that were being affected with the bizarre, pain-inflicting condition. From north of Bergen and Sundre to the south of Elkford and right down to Little Bow Provincial Park, reports were filed. It always happened in the same way, groups of similar type animals were found dead or dying from intense pain. Witnesses always reported the hideous screaming that went along with it. At first, it seemed that no type of animal was safe, but cows were rarely affected. Horses were always affected. The thing about horses is that they are very intuitive, able to sense trouble or danger. They become nervous, and their fear can cause problems that horse-hands and vets watch for, and that became a major difficulty for ranchers like Ben Gasner. Not all of his horses had been affected by the killer, but they were all terrified. The horses felt fear and started reacting in bizarre ways, laying off their feed, nipping at one another's legs, purposely injuring themselves. Havoc was reigning on Ben's ranch, and elsewhere.

Eventually, the killer zeroed-in on domestic animals, though again, quite selectively. It was killing cats and dogs. And it was no longer focused on rural areas between Calgary and the Rockies. Reports had come in from city dwellers frantically trying to help their suffering pets. High River, Olds, Airdrie, Strathmore and Calgary were all included. Cats by the dozens were encountered on the city streets. Both pets and strays were found wailing and screeching as if hot pokers had been laid upon them. Anxiety struck the half-million feline population. Fear drove the animals mad, and pet-owners were helpless. But, to many, it seemed even harder on dogs. Howling and whimpering filled the air as canines everywhere exhibited strange fits of pain.

If this thing was a disease, it was jumping species: we had seen it go from the raccoons to livestock, and now to the cats and dogs. It seemed focused, as if by plan and purpose. And the damnedest thing of all was that the veterinary and medical fields were completely helpless. Nothing could be pinpointed. All we knew was that the nervous systems of the targeted animals were being maxed out as if by electrical voltage or some other increasingly intense stimulation.

The observations were always the same: the animal undergoes the period of agony that lasted several hours. Regardless of the animal, it seemed that death seldom occurred in less time. The animals always remained conscious throughout the ordeal: they never blacked out. Further injuries were sustained through the fits and gnashing that the animal experienced in its contortions: sprained muscles; internal hemorrhaging; swallowing or biting off their own tongues; bleeding through the eyes, ears and nose; vomiting and defecating; and finally towards the end, brain embolisms — and death.

By the latter part of August the papers were reporting that the killer was costing tens of millions of dollars, to say nothing of the emotional and physical carnage. But it still hadn't reared its ugly head outside the province — and that was odd. It hadn't crossed the boundary of the Rocky Mountains, nor had it swung as far north as Red Deer or south to Lethbridge. Was it contained? There was no answer. No one knew what the hell it was. The authorities were completely lost. It was as if the fourth horseman of the apocalypse had galloped across the foothills of Alberta and laid waste the animals.

Most of the province's dailies covered the events in their own style and manner. A story appearing in The Journal reported a "mutated form of rabies threatening animal husbandry." The Herald ran a number of smaller pieces about "farmers' threat moving into city" and "species jumping killer threatening animal welfare." The Sun, in its typical simple-minded style cited "sizzling bacon" in reference to swine being affected and "Old MacDonald's Bad Ol' Farm" regarding farmer and rancher nightmares in struggling with the onslaught. There was nothing funny about what was happening.

Rumours ran rampant that we were in the midst of some military test field gone awry. No one would confirm it, but there was also talk of U.S. specialists and military in the area studying and trying to contain the zone. Yet, no one knew what it was. It got to a point where news items were being controlled, perhaps to avoid the chance of widespread panic. And that was the real basis of the fear, wasn't it?

After all, how much panic would you expect regarding a disease that attacked only animals. Not much, not unless you thought it might cross the next barrier: the barrier into human race.

And that's exactly where it was headed.

It's always amazing the clarity that hindsight seems to provide. This thing was targeting various sorts of animals within an area less than one tenth the size of Alberta. It had moved from species to species. It focused on small — then larger — groups at a single time. It delivered a result — pain — over a few hours. It led its victims to death, but only after the animals' bodies were "burned out," when they couldn't take any more.

Some people started putting their animals down before the thing even hit them. Many ranchers shot their own horses and dogs in the midst of their suffering. Fear and confusion had already run its course into the human race. The mystery killer was attacking the animals, but now the humans were being affected in a different manner. Anguish and helplessness led to cases of depression, suicide, and various forms of chaos. The researchers, scientists, and Ph.Ds were finding nothing. Nothing! With as many resources and minds as were being centralized on the killer, nothing had been discovered.

But business had to go on. Ben had lost a number horses and ponies to the killer and events were serious, but there was business to run and whatever was happening would eventually be sorted out, God willing. In the meantime, income had to be strategized for the future. Ben sent me out east — to Toronto — trusting me to close a couple of futures trade deals. The specifics of the futures are not important, but Ben obviously hoped to make gains over the next few years from the deals.

The time away would be good for me. I needed the emotional distance from all that was happening out west. Plus, the trip was only for three days and the deals went well, so that aspect of things was easy enough.

It was Saturday afternoon when I arrived back at Calgary's international airport. Jordan had made the arrangement to pick me up and we made good time getting onto Crowchild Trail and back to the ranch. Conversation centered primarily on what had transpired on my trip, and as well, I wanted to keep current with any further updates in the area.

"Nothin's improved much," Jordan declared.

"We'll get through this," I said, but I'm not sure I meant it.

We pulled into the main part of the ranch at about 6:40 p.m. Laura was just in the process of preparing supper for Ben, Jordan and myself, knowing that I was arriving back. Ben looked especially haggard. The events were taking their toll on him, but I sensed that Laura had been supportive of him.

Ben and I sat down for about 20 minutes to review the futures contracts. Then it was time for supper, and I shared a bit of news about Toronto with each of them over the dinner table. Laura and Ben were both oddly silent. Things seemed so grave.

"What is it?" I asked, fully expecting the answer I received.

"We've lost more livestock in the few days you've been away. Most people are ready to look for any kind of explanation to this mystery."

Then Laura hit me with a bomb.

"Did you get much of our news out east?" she asked.

I replied that I hadn't.

"Well," she continued, "the news is that the hospitals are seeing an increase in their emergency wards. People are complaining of increased aches and pains, but we're being told it's a psychosomatic reaction to what the animals have been experiencing."

"What?!" I said. "They don't even know what this thing is yet, so how can they be so sure it hasn't stepped into the human population?"

"They'd never report it so quick even if they knew it had crossed over," Ben stated. "I'm sure the authorities are very much aware of what's happening."

We suddenly became very quiet at the table. The significance of what this could mean was numbing. We chatted a bit more over dinner that evening. Then, we each pitched in to clean up and I finally left the room.

The days passed, and the inevitable happened. Local news reported what Laura had mentioned that evening over supper: hospitals were receiving a plethora of admittals for numerous complaints. Many would be legit, but so many more were psychosomatic. People's fears were getting ahead of them. Trepidation of what might be was creating its own secular reality. And then the real attack came.

Jordan came flying through the door late one afternoon with the news. A cattle rancher near Waiparous had been found dead along with his two sons and an unidentified woman. It was Gene Templeton. The bodies had been discovered by his wife. There was evidence of a struggle at the scene, but that, in fact, was a sign of their violent death throes. Their eardrums had been shattered. Blood had coagulated heavily around the eyes. Each dying man had tried to get help, or make it to a phone, but their agonies halted them. Each had ultimately died of heart attack. But how long did it take for their hearts to give out? There was no question in Jordan's mind what had killed them. After he relayed the story, there wasn't any doubt in Laura's mind or my own either. Ben hadn't been there to hear it, he was out looking after the horses. Though they hadn't been friends, Ben had known Gene for years.

Medical autopsies were performed. But the news already made its way by word of mouth across the area. People didn't wait for the official cause of death, instead they drew their own conclusions. Jordan left as quickly as he came. Laura and I found ourselves embracing each other. We were scared.

The evening news mentioned the deaths without

much detail. Within the next few days, reports of seizures and deaths started to come in furiously. It all happened in the same general area. The bizarre killer had been reported to the north of Raven, east to Three Hills and as far south as the Crowsnest Pass. It was now striking small groups of people in rural areas, much the same way it began with the animals. But the tempo had increased. It was targeting a broader circle of victims and striking more and more over a wider area than it had with the animals. Panic set in. Many families simply up and left the area, heading south to the United States or as far east as they could go.

Small communities had been completely wiped out. The details were always gruesome. Bodies crashed and bled-out; victims always hemorrhaged heavily; some gouged themselves in the throes of death; pregnant mothers aborted. Always, there was death. Hospitals were being inundated. Emergency services were overworked. Local mayors and the premier declared a state of emergency. But there was a problem: there was no way to know when the killer would strike — or where.

Pandemonium had begun.

First hit were areas like Riverbend and Douglasdale: small neighbourhoods on the outer perimeter of the city. Then we heard about hundreds of people being stricken in areas closer to the core; Woodbine, Oak Ridge and Lakeview. Roads were closed. Emergency medical teams and special first-aid tents were set up throughout town. Riot squads stood on alert. The mayor even imposed a 10 o'clock curfew to help control the hysteria.

Word spread that we were being hit with some 20th-century plague, but nothing could be validated: no vermin were identified as carriers. No germ or microbe could be found. The search continued to find the source of the brutal killer. People were now suffering and dying in droves. We were seeing people writhing on the street — with no means of help.

Inevitably, it hit home. The four of us had kept ourselves busy in our vigil of trying to run the ranch despite the turmoil. Then, one Thursday afternoon, we were going to gather in the house for a midday break.

"Where's Ben?" Laura asked after the three of us had waited for close to half an hour.

"Hell," Jordan said. "I left him at the livery stable, he was right behind me."

"We better check," I suggested.

"Yeah," Jordan said, and the two of us went outside to the stable.

And that was the day that everything in our lives blew apart. There is little more for me to say. Nothing was ever the same again. We found Ben — he was delirious, screaming, passing out, coming to again, begging us to help him. His face was crimson red. He was covered in sweat and blisters that looked like boils, with blood coming from his ears and eyes. I'll never forget, especially his pleas for us to help him.

He was begging us for help and there was nothing we could do.

In my heart I've forgiven Jordan. He simply decided he'd had enough and ran. For the rest of my days I'll remember the look in Jordan's eyes as we each stood by completely helpless watching Ben Gasner die.

This tale might have gone a thousand different ways. It could have ended in the extinction of the human species — but it didn't. It might have developed as one of the greatest tragedies of the 20th century, but that is not the case either. Perhaps it could have finished by wiping out half the western world, or the entire population of western Canada — but that didn't happen.

Towards what may have been our end, and before death had spread elsewhere, I wonder now if we were saved by the simplest of virtues. Certainly, at a point when no answers were available, we must ask ourselves "what really happened here?" and "what saved us?"

You see, I wonder this, and I ask these questions because of something I had kept to myself: something that troubled my thoughts, my sleep, and to some degree, even my conscience for keeping to myself what I must now reveal.

It was seemingly insignificant — nothing more than mere speculation if it carried any merit at all. It occurred during my trip to Toronto.

The plan was that I would only be in Toronto for

three days at best, though I had the flexibility to stay longer if the business dealings required it. What transpired took place on a Wednesday afternoon after I finished lunch in a small restaurant off Bay and Front Streets in Toronto. Not having been in the city for some years, I had gone for a walk through the financial district until I connected with Yonge St. It was here, at a small newsstand, that I stopped and purchased a copy of Voice — a small alternative newspaper that serves a relatively small readership within the city.

There, was what might seem to be a ludicrous article meant only as a gag; the type you'd typically see on covers of cheap state-side tabloids. The title was: "Manifestations Turn Killer Out West."

It was crazy, to be sure. After all, we've all seen tabloids that declare all sorts of wild things we take to be fiction and nothing else. But someone had written an article specifically about the tragedies out west.

The article focused on an interview with scientific and paranormal researcher Ken Kincardine, who travelled the world extensively but lived in Seattle. He had visited Toronto for a week in late August when a freelance writer did the interview with him. What Kincardine claimed was astonishing. Few people would ever believe it, but it focused on the situation in Alberta. The article indicated he had learned about the turmoil in Alberta during the latter part of July, though at that point, very little had been written about it. Kincardine hypothesized that "fears and anxieties had manifested into physical carnage which developed its own consciousness". This consciousness literally fed on the torment and pain caused by physical suffering, thus creating its own vicious circle. Pain was initially focused on lesser groups of life forms — animals. This 'super mind' created physical agony, and then lapped-up "psychic turmoils" as nourishment. It was as if an entirely new consciousness had been created — or attracted — to then propagate and further its own insatiable appetite for wonton suffering.

I read the article in its entirety. It was quite beyond my scope of belief. Who would believe it? Yet, I remember once having read of an American reporter who wrote successfully on minor articles he picked up in daily newspapers. These small 50 word articles spoke of entire French towns gone insane and stories about UFO abductions which led to some very fascinating and factually based stories. I therefore decided not to totally dismiss Kincardine and the Voice interview.

I bought a few more copies of the publication and went straight to a pay phone. It was my intention to first speak to the reporter of the article, and if possible, track down Mr. Kincardine.

After reaching someone in Voice's editorial department, I was told I would have to leave my name and number for the writer of the article, which I did. Realizing there was little else I could do for the time being, I scoured a few more news stands looking for additional references to the Alberta incidents. I found a number of articles, but nothing beyond my own knowledge of the situation. I thought it best that I return to my hotel room and wait for a call, realizing however that it may never come.

To my surprise, a call did come that evening. A young lady by the name of Ginette Walters had written the article, and Ginette was completely sold on the authenticity of Ken Kincardine's theories. Kincardine apparently had a reputation for helping stateside police departments. He had recently been instrumental in identifying and apprehending a serial rapist in Washington state. In '87 he had been the key person in locating two missing boys in one of our national parks. Both kids had been near their end when Kincardine directed the search parties into a small culvert that he had described perfectly from the meager evidence and a somewhat psychic bent. The boys were saved. Numerous other predictions of Kincardine's had also come true. Many of his visions and insights had been authenticated. Typically, he chose to stay out of the limelight. Ginette never gave any reason for his willingness to do the Voice interview.

During that interview, he described how this super-consciousness would grow and develop like disease. He claimed it would destroy life in its quest for its strange psychic nourishment, which it assimilated through the pain and torment of physical beings. Even though he had been asked during the interview, he had no advice on how to defeat it. He did, however, have some insight: this thing was "brought" upon us, and feelings of fear and anguish would only contribute to its growth and strength.

It was an astonishing story. Ginette was completely convinced of the man's authenticity. So why not get the word out? Why not spread the news of this incredible insight? It's not hard to understand. Ginette had approached over 15 different dailies and several magazines with her story. But she was virtually laughed at. No respectable publication would touch her story. It was right up there with alien abductions and sightings of giant sea monsters.

Yet, something about it struck a chord in me. My next step would be to see if I could convince Ginette to give me Kincardine's address or phone number.

"Well," Ginette said, "I'd provide it to you if only I had it — I don't."

"Oh?"

"But not to worry," she continued, "I know that he's gone to Vancouver, he said he would be staying at the downtown Regency. You'll find him there easily enough for the next week or so."

I thanked her and finished our call.

By that time, I had to conclude my pursuit of Kincardine in order to finalize my business dealings for Ben. I therefore completed the remainder of business and was back in Calgary by 5 p.m. that Saturday. Though, while in Toronto, I had taken the trouble to get the Vancouver Regency phone number and Kincardine's room number. Fortunately, the hotel had no instructions against letting his name out. I placed two separate calls to the man but was unable to reach him, and rather than leave a message, I decided to try a few more times to see if I could get him in person.

By the time I tried him again I was back at the ranch and it would have been approaching 7:30 p.m. in Vancouver. To my surprise, I got him on the line that evening. After making a humble introduction, I found Kincardine surprisingly open about speaking with me. As we got onto the topic of my call, his tone and demeanour became very grave. He was absolutely serious with what he had stated for the Voice interview.

It startles the mind to conceive of just what he was suggesting. This thing had developed from simple negative feelings into a growing, functioning entity. A parasite, he called it. And really, what else would it be? It created the conditions by which it fed: dark energies, all of which came from pain — and the ultimate death — of living things.

What did it look like? We would never see it. It was not here in a way we understood. He painted it as evil, or a manifestation that grew from such things. It created the conditions it needed, but negative reactions to it would only help it grow and multiply. Feelings of fear and anger would seduce it, make it stronger.

If he was right, it would be parasitic if it existed at all. I found myself being seduced into the thought that it might really exist. Kincardine was able to offer little advice on what to do to rid ourselves of the invader. But he did focus on the principle of its existence: it was attracted by feelings of fear and anxiety. I asked if he had approached any of the authorities with his impressions. He claimed he had tried to a limited degree, but was met with ridicule. I chose not to go into it any further. I understood.

There was no reason why I should have chosen to believe Kincardine's story, except for the fact that there were no other explanations, no other theories. Science was not finding the reason for the horrible death. No one had any answers, and at the time it seemed that the move was being made into the human population.

Kincardine and I spoke no further that evening, nor ever again. I decided to keep my conversation with him to myself and did not inform Ben or Laura. What would be the point? There was no proof. There could be no validation. I wasn't even sure I believed it. It all seemed so preposterous, and yet...

I spent the following nights in fitful attempts to rest. The imagination wanders. I found myself conjuring up visions of hideous blood-sucking monstrosities: things that manifested and then vanished. Life robbers. The nights outside seemed oddly quiet. I got up and stared into my mirror. It was as if a hundred featureless faces gazed back at me, all of them wanting, all of them hungry. Suddenly it was just my face being reflected back to me. I shuddered, and tried again to sleep. I spent most of my evenings in a state between wakefulness and sleep, where reality is not concrete. When I did sleep, I would jolt awake with ugly things sliding down my walls. Nightmares. How many people would be affected by their own fears of what was happening? Anxiety would be a certainty. I suffered from it that night and during that entire awful time. How could one not? But I kept it in. I kept it all in.

And so Kincardine's message never really got out. The story out east never drew attention. Ginette Walter's article fell on deaf ears. And I too was guilty of keeping what I had discovered all to myself in defiance of my own fear of humiliation and doubt.

Thus the end approached. In the final hours, no one was prepared to survive. Fear had engulfed us all. Only small portions of the region continued to function. Few businesses continued to operate. Local dailies were published only sporadically. But in the end, it seems that there was one message that shone through for each of us. This is what I find to be curious, for I wonder if we weren't rescued by this one saving grace.

It was the message our spiritual messiahs have been telling us for centuries; the very same one you see plastered on billboards as you drive down your local freeway; the exact message our churches and evangelists have been sending us for years: *love thy neighbour.*

Was that it? Was that our saving grace? I don't know.

Ken Kincardine said we were being visited and

preyed upon. He stated that our unseen visitor fed on our fears, and in turn brought about greater fear and doubt by the physical anguish it created. But love conquers fear. Anger and desperation are based on fear, and love conquers all. Is there any other explanation? Was that it? In the end, there was no future, there was no hope. I was there. I know.

It was our darkest hour. We were beaten. With nothing to hope for and nothing to expect other than doom, an incredible thing happened. Buried in despair and without hope, we gave up our fates to the unseen destroyer. There was nothing left to do. In that one final day, that one final hour, our simple human hearts came to accept our fate and turned the last fledgling bit of feelings in our hearts to each other. In our greatest time of crisis, our love for each other endured — stronger than before.

Then? Nothing. As mysteriously as the grim killer had appeared, so now did it vanish and disperse like some dark cloud blown back by a greater force. Now a burden was lifted from us. Now our fears and anger were gone.

And yet I ask myself: were we really visited? Was something unworldly and sinister really targeting us? I doubt we will ever know. If Kincardine was right, if we really did help ourselves in our last moments of hopeless desperation with love and prayer, then we must surely give thought to these things. For whatever the circumstances, and whatever the ends, we must consider the power behind such thoughts. And we certainly must give thought to the consequences of absence of such thoughts.

I've stayed on the ranch with Laura. Despite what you might think, we are just friends, but we are good friends. Both our hearts and the ranch have needed much healing, and much of the future hangs in limbo. Time, they say, can cure all things. We shall see.

I will often wonder about what happened here. Why this, I wonder? Why now? If such a thing as Kincardine's demon can exist, then why wouldn't it have chosen the deeper, darker city cores of Los Angeles? Or New York? Or Chicago? Why wouldn't it have chosen one of the many desperate and squalid locations of the Third World? Of India? Or Nigeria? Why not the U.K.? Perhaps it has. Perhaps it does. We certainly read about enough scourges around the globe. So few of these things are ever really solved, or cured. And what about the ones we don't read about? I wonder if such blights could be vehicles for greater, darker purposes. I wonder if, this time, it was just experimenting; getting ready, preparing for an even greater assault. And — in the end — I wonder if it's all our choice.

I wonder.

BEYOND THE GLADE

In cold grey landscapes of eons-old deadwood and remnant charred woods left standing from fires long ago gone; in hillsides of wilted yellow grass and sandy ash blown wide from tall cold dunes a hundred miles west; in twilights of bitter cold horizons and dull billowing clouds which seldom seemed to change: this is how I remember that place where he came and he dwelt. 'Twas the canvas of early life; that place of youth and adolescence that slides into the hidden archetypes of our subconscious from that state of consciousness, be it real or otherwise perceived.

Thus was my childhood and the memories of that time and place: dark, cold, grey, bleak. Though this is not the reality of how my early years began — of that I am sure. For I remember green spruce and cobalt blue skies that carried songbirds under the warm radiance of Sol: alive and joyous in its overseeing grandeur of creation. Yet, it was somewhere along this time and place that he came. And so then did the memory of those greener things remembered transform themselves into a vile cavity of indescribable coldness.

All was very simply the far-reaching rural stage of happy children born only to taste and sample the eternity of spring: Spring-fed water holes, the beauty of blossoms, the green of pastures and the out-lying forest; of happiness and the love of families and the bond of church and community and our one little schoolhouse. We frolicked and played and knew only simple virtues and the blessed moment of being, all in a place isolated in time, removed to its own inlet of bliss, and then — he was there.

A youth much like ourselves, though different in some strange way: red-haired, with sharp, unpleasant features and cold, hollow eyes. Not a handsome youth and always very odd and peculiar in a manner we could not comprehend. He came daily to the little school house and played alone outside the periphery of our games. At the end of each day he would disappear beyond the glade to a place where all could only assume dwelt his kin. Gradually, however though gradually, he came to be accepted within our little circle of peers, yet though we included him there was always that feeling of unease and trepidation in our young hearts for reasons we could not identify.

The years went by and many of us grew close as would be reasoned. He was there though always separate and apart in his strange and removed manner. His time around us, however, softened and so reduced the feelings of peculiarity we had for him, that for a period he became known as "friend."

It is not for me to say the year, but it happened as with all great mysteries known not of this earth that the devastating tragedies and bleak occurrences ran rampant through our cherished little community: select certain of the young people began disappearing. It is that form of mystery and chaos that lends itself to the worst of nightmares; those things that bare down heaviest upon the families and friends of those gone missing. For in not knowing the fate of missing youth is an ever bitter and oppressing blanket of wrath borne from the depths of disparity and fear for unbeknownst natures and darkness of fates.

Over several years, as if something were selecting choice morsels of victims in the guise of children, the disappearances continued. Authorities were at their wits' end to find so much as a single clue. Not one hair, not one footprint, not a single article of clothing was found. Trackers sought out wild beasts — of hoof or of claw or foot — but no killer nor suspect was ever found. The woods grew still, as if in quieting of screams that must have nestled upon the mouths and minds of the families of those absconded. A once blessed and blissful little inlet from a farther-reaching maddening world had now itself tasted madness. Yet over this vast period of frantic sorrow, life was forced to continue. For with each case of a missing child, it was always hoped that it would be the last and final one. But the children continued to disappear. And so this malevolent and macabre bleak cloud persisted for years, gradually draining the life from the once happy little area and replacing it instead with a soured bitter venom that eased into the very heart of the wood, the water, and the land until a grey pallor fell upon the face of the Earth itself.

Yet many stayed, for this was the place where ancestral roots were laid and families were raised.

It was during a late autumn that I bore witness to that which should not have been observed with earthly eyes. It was that place where destruction of mind seeps into the realities of our world which we all hold so dear, imagined or real as I now claim them to be. I had friends with whom he played, of this I have already made clear. But during this one late fall it was these friends who now fell prey to that unsolved riddle, the void of disappearance. One by one, the few of us that once remained were now gone without so much as a clue.

Betwixt the tears, the anguish of heart, the gnashing of teeth and mind for the presumed downed and vanished friends, he was still there and about in his odd and peculiar manner of indifference and coyness. It would not have been but for a moment of chance that I noticed two of my friends had been with him before vanishing. And so, though I never took it upon myself to so much as warn anyone of my deep and heartfelt suspicions, I kept to myself my frantic and curious dread of thought. Yet, it was when I saw him with a third friend — a young lady of 14 or 15 — that I took it upon myself to watch and observe in the greatest secrecy and cleverest of stealth.

'Twas toward the end of day, before the grey sky gave over to the bleak cavity of night, that I saw her unwittingly accompany him to his destination beyond the glade. I followed, though from a fairly great distance so that I maintained a pace of several minutes behind them, yet strong on their trail without arousing suspicion. Long they walked into the forest, passed the culverts, along the creek beds, up through the winding hillside, and then to a flattened portion of ground where it was known that still waters lay. It was at this point that I momentarily lost their track — though only momentarily.

And ah! For in the shadows, as I crept over a steep hillside in the greatest of quiet, I beheld that which defies all rationale, yet succumbs to complete feelings of dread. A shudder ran through my every limb, as if my spine itself were amassed with countless unknown sensations of terror and loathing, for I was paralyzed in a way that only insurmountable fear can freeze one. The terrain was surreal: cold, still and vacant, as if I had stumbled onto a vacuum within this forest that defied creation. My eyes beheld terror, numb and nauseating, and I was again like a child too weak to move, too stricken with fear to turn away. I lay, atop the hillside, peering down while an unholy chill kept me immobile, and I knew then that there are those things in the cosmos that man should not know, was not designed to understand, nor ever deemed capable of comprehending. For this I saw:

There, below, was a large grey pool which at one time would have been blue and clean and teeming with life, but now lay tepid and vile; sterile and cold. There was not the slightest breeze and the air was stale with the putrid heaviness of death: or that which does not live. The region was without colour as a man's eye might understand colour: as bleak and empty as the dull hue of old ice, yet colder still. Not a single leaf hung from the deadwood which surrounded the rancid unholy place. The soil? — like ash. And the stillness of the area defied being, for there was no life — none.

And then I saw, and my eyes must have been lit ablaze. I do not know if I screamed, but in my mind I heard an echoing chorus of screams. And they were the screams of many: legions of voices, all rampant with unknown pain and anguish of terror. And then again I heard only silence, so pure that it seemed not a single soul nor bit of life ever stepped into this place.

There, in the mirror-still surface of the grey bed of water, I saw a vision of him: a dweller from the other side; a place of netherworlds. 'Twas as if a doorway opened and closed on that mirror-still body of water: as if it was his gate to a place where only hopelessness is emitted and of which a man's mind cannot fathom. I saw him, disappearing downward as still and lifeless as those things surrounding him. His face was still, dead, lifeless, unmoving, with eyes that held a stillness that belayed anti-life. And with him I saw her: screaming, alive, frozen with the knowledge of her onset of doom, for she must have known of the terrible place where she was destined. I saw them sink into this place as my heart sought to leap from my chest. And then I did scream, for before the mirrored-doorway disappeared and again became the dead still surface of water, he reappeared from that place and gazed on me with hollow dead eyes and a single spoken word. Then he was gone. And the doorway was closed forever.

I left the memories and the years behind me. To

the towering concrete monuments of our modern cities I fled, forever in a quest to forget and bury in my mind that which I would prefer to believe I did not witness. Into the future of my years I ran, forever seeking to dull my senses and forget. But there has been no relief, no forgetting, no solace, for my years have contained a stillness all their own, and the vision of him has carried with me.

There is a point of resignation to the dying; of fatalism known to the wild animal trapped and bound for destruction. Yet, at this point of certainty there lies that place outside the peripheries of all senses, all realities. It is a place beyond the wall of sanity and knowing. For although these things may be based on the frailties of the mind, there are things and places which man is not equipped to fathom. Yes, the years have sped by, and I have been many places: all in futile attempts to escape and forget. But such has not been meant for me. For increasingly, he has been with me. Through my dreams at night, and in my thoughts of each waking day, he has accompanied me, followed me, and I know that whatever he may be he is real. He has come for me.

The vision in my mind is always the same. I see that rancid surface of dead still water: that doorway to the place where he is the bringer; that place which is the other side of being, that prison of no hope. He is there, gazing back at me, with eyes dead and wanting, and a single spoken word...

"Soon."

FERGUS' JOB

Amid the carnage, the broken bodies, strewn limbs, all the entrails and bits and pieces of every conceivable body part; fragments of bone and gristle and dried baked blood — there, he sat. And loomed. It was a delightful place. Screams of perpetual agony filled the air. Shrieks and groans simply never ended, and would never end. And the stench of smouldering, burnt skin wafted upward to linger forever in the hot, putrid air. But the high-pitched screams of unimaginable searing agony really were the best. Yes, Fergus really did have it pretty good.

But alas, boredom had finally begun to set in. And why not? After all, it had been well before the beginning of time itself that Fergus had held this most prestigious post. In fact, Fergus had sat there patiently from the very beginning, waiting for the first of the souls to arrive. And through all the millennia of time he really had become quite proficient at his work. Fergus knew and performed his job very, very well.

And The Master liked him. Much earlier, in the before time, Fergus had actually dared to boast how he would thrust the mighty spit through The Master himself and let the old fart roast forever over the eternal flame. Word of this quickly made way through the upper echelons of the hierarchy and found its way to him. What followed still remains legend. The Master let out such a wail of a howl upon hearing Fergus' intent, that every slimy and slithery thing hastened in quick retreat to the darkest shadows and deepest coves. All but Fergus. Fergus propped himself up against a hot rock, threw one leg over the other, and began to pick his teeth lazily. This so enraged The Master that he nearly lost all control. And The Master liked that. Anyone who could send *him* into such a tither over such a daring taunt and yet remain so indifferent and calm was definitely worth his salt in this place. Yes, Fergus was on his way. And so it was that Fergus was given this most important job.

Fergus gently rotated the spit and reflected. Flames shot upward and the typical unearthly, insane scream followed — as always. Fergus managed a wry smile and reminisced... it really had been so, so long. So many bodies and so many souls had come and gone under his little domain. Now, rows and rows of those waiting to experience his special talents waited in lines that seemed to extend to the horizons of forever. But the lure and enjoyment was no more. Perhaps after all this time and all those souls, Fergus had just become burned out. Was it possible? He recalled the simple little glee he once felt — long ago — with every new job that came before him. (Fergus had come to call each soul a "job," since he always felt that each and every one deserved his complete and undivided attention.)

Souls — bodies: metaphysical extensions of the physical. What did it matter now anyway? Most of the fun had gone. Gone was the joy of thrusting the spit. Gone was the challenge of encouraging the wildest scream. Gone was the simple pleasure in watching charred remains fall from the spit into the eternal depths forever.

Once, in earlier times (when the system was still under review), Fergus reached over to discover... a saint! Now, sometimes, this was still known to happen. But Fergus never gave much consideration to this, after all, Fergus wasn't Administration. Nevertheless, nothing — absolutely nothing — was more joyous than watching the expression on the face of someone who, least of all though expecting to end up here, now faced Fergus and his little workshop. (Especially a saint.)

Fergus casually took the next in line and prepared to thrust the spit. This part could be tricky. Sometimes, if you cast the spit just right, you could drive it directly through the spine and create the most interesting effect. Oh, the screaming was something to behold all right. But better yet, it made the neatest little popping sounds — just like a row of chestnuts all bursting open on a hot summer's day. Fergus still liked that.

This time, however, he was off by just that much.

It didn't matter. It really didn't make any difference any more. He had had it! After an infinity of time, Fergus had finally hit tilt. Enough was enough. Sure, he could cast a spit and perform a roast like no other, but now it was time for new horizons — new endeavours. Time to reach outward and move upward!

Even from before the beginning, when Fergus started here, The Master had been The Master and nothing had ever happened to change that! But even for *him* there must come a time to move over — a time to make way for newer and more inspired leadership!

Fergus could feel himself getting hotter and hotter as he dwelled on it. No one had seen more of The Damned than Fergus. No one had done as much or worked as hard to maintain the reputation of this regime. And, certainly, no one had developed more experience in the damning process than he. Let some other insipid little demon take over at the spit. Fergus had paid his dues! A promotion was in order, and Fergus was good and ready to have it happen now!

Fergus practically caught himself spinning the spit in his state of heightened anger and quickly relented. Relax, there would be time. Time, time, time. In fact, in this place, there was nothing but time. When the vortex and continuum of eternity itself folded over and forever ceased to exist, there would still be time. Yes, and Fergus would be ready. Ready to take control of what would then be his kingdom. Ready to play his part in the onset of a totally new time. Ready to assign some eager little imp to the role of this workshop. And ready to greet the completely new and uninitiated batch of The Damned.

Yes, all this Fergus would do. But for the time being, for now, Fergus would wait. Fergus would wait and continue as before, as always, until he could wait no more.

And so, for now...

"Next, please."

Pressed-To-Tell Publications
P.O. Box 455
31 Adelaide Street East
Toronto, Ontario
M5C 2J5

Toll free: 1-888-272-2152